HOW WE ROLL

HOW
WE
ROLL

NATASHA FRIEND

SQUARE FISH

FARRAR STRAUS GIROUX
NEW YORK

SQUARE
FISH

An imprint of Macmillan Publishing Group, LLC
120 Broadway, New York, NY 10271
fiercereads.com

Square Fish and the Square Fish logo are trademarks of Macmillan and
are used by Farrar Straus Giroux under license from Macmillan.

Our books may be purchased in bulk for promotional, educational, or business use. Please
contact your local bookseller or the Macmillan Corporate and Premium Sales Department
at (800) 221-7945 ext. 5442 or by email at MacmillanSpecialMarkets@macmillan.com.

Library of Congress Cataloging-in-Publication Data

Names: Friend, Natasha, 1972– author.
Title: How we roll / by Natasha Friend.
Description: | New York : Farrar Straus Giroux, 2018. | Summary:
    After developing alopecia Quinn lost her friends along with her hair and former
    football player Jake lost his legs and confidence after an accident, but the two
    help each other believe in themselves and the possibility of love.
Identifiers: LCCN 2017042313 | ISBN 978-1-250-30881-8 (paperback) |
    ISBN 978-0-374-30567-3 (ebook)
Subjects: | CYAC: Self-acceptance—Fiction. | Alopecia areata—Fiction. |
    Amputees—Fiction. | People with disabilities—Fiction. | Dating
    (Social customs)—Fiction. | Family life—Massachusetts—Fiction. |
    Massachusetts—Fiction.
Classification: LCC PZ7.F91535 How 2018 | DDC [Fic]—dc23
LC record available at https://lccn.loc.gov/2017042313

Originally published in the United States by Farrar Straus Giroux
First Square Fish edition, 2019
Book designed by Elizabeth H. Clark
Square Fish logo designed by Filomena Tuosto

7 9 10 8 6

LEXILE: HL570L

For Sanah

Hard is trying to rebuild yourself, piece by piece, with no instruction book, and no clue as to where all the important bits are supposed to go.

—NICK HORNBY, *A LONG WAY DOWN*

HOW WE ROLL

PROLOGUE

ON THE FIRST DAY OF SEVENTH GRADE, Quinn, Paige, and Tara wore matching outfits. Oxford shirts, capri jeans, Keds. They took turns sitting on a stool in Paige's kitchen while Paige's mom did their hair. Three matching French braids, three matching bows. None of this had been Quinn's call. Truthfully, she thought the triplets idea was stupid, but she didn't feel strongly enough to protest. She just rolled with it, the same way she'd rolled with playing Barbies and building fairy houses and watching *Disney on Ice*—all the things Paige and Tara had liked when they were little.

"Let's go to the skate park," Quinn had suggested once. She'd gotten a skateboard for her eleventh birthday, the same birthday Julius had ruined by smashing Quinn's cake.

"The skate park?" Paige repeated.

"Yeah," Quinn said. "It'll be fun."

"You're the only one with a skateboard," Tara said.

"We can take turns," Quinn said.

But Paige wrinkled her nose, and Tara said, "I don't think my mom wants to drive us to the skate park. Let's do pedicures."

Well, what was Quinn supposed to do? It was Tara's house, Tara's rules. Just like when they went to Paige's house, it was Paige's rules. It never worked that way at Quinn's house. At Quinn's house, it was Julius's rules. Everyone knew that, which was why they never went there.

From the time Julius had had his first meltdown, Quinn's mother called one of two people: Paige's mom or Tara's mom. "Can Quinn come over for a while?" And they always said of course. Paige's house and Tara's house became Quinn's houses, too. If Quinn had to estimate, she would say that she'd spent at least 38 percent of seventh grade sleeping over in the Braskys' basement or the Patlases' guest room.

Eighth grade was a different story. There were no matching outfits. For one thing, Quinn had no hair left to French braid. But also, Paige and Tara started wearing crazy clothes. Like push-up bras. And tube tops, these stretchy pieces of fabric that barely covered their belly buttons.

Quinn didn't know how it had happened. Sometime over the summer, while she'd been dribbling her basketball, Paige and Tara had been taking secret trips to the Pearl Street Mall, double piercing their ears and stockpiling spandex.

On the first day of eighth grade, Quinn showed up on

Paige's doorstep wearing her favorite basketball shorts and her Colorado Rockies baseball cap. When the door opened, Quinn laughed. Paige and Tara looked like two of Beyoncé's backup singers about to take the stage.

"What are you *wearing*?" Quinn said.

"What are *you* wearing?" Paige said.

Tara looked Quinn up and down. She shook her head. "Seriously, Quinn?"

"What?" Quinn said.

"We're in eighth grade now."

"So?"

"So," Paige said, "you're dressed like a fifth-grade boy."

"Would you rather I go to school like this?" Quinn took off her Colorado Rockies baseball cap. There was only one tiny scraggle of hair left by then, holding on for dear life.

She remembered the looks on their faces.

No. God, no. Don't go to school like that.

"I didn't think so," Quinn said. She put her hat back on.

CHAPTER

1

ON THE FIRST MORNING OF HER NEW LIFE, Quinn was debating. Guinevere or Sasha? Guinevere was long, strawberry blond, and wavy. Sasha was short and black, glossy as a patent-leather shoe. They were Estetica human hair wigs, $2,000 a pop, no joke. They lived on two Styrofoam heads on Quinn's dresser. They were supposed to make her feel normal. Right.

G. I. Jane.

Hare Krishna.

Professor X.

Quinn looked at her reflection. Most of the time she tried not to, but today she looked. You would think that after 408 days she'd be used to it. She wasn't. She was a cue ball. A plucked chicken. Her mirror hadn't been hung up yet. It was propped on three cardboard boxes that she had yet to unpack.

Maybe she would do it later, put her new room together. Or maybe she would live out of cardboard boxes like a nomad until her parents came to their senses—until they realized that loading all their earthly possessions into a U-Haul and driving two thousand miles wasn't going to change anything. What was that expression? *Wherever you go, there you are?*

It had been a week, and so far they were still here. Gulls Head, Massachusetts, which was a weird name for a town. Even weirder was the accent everyone seemed to have. The real estate agent, the cashier at 7-Eleven, the secretary from Gulls Head High School who'd given Quinn a tour. Everyone in this town talked like the letter *R* didn't exist. *Far* was "fah." *Locker* was "lockah." *How are you?* sounded like "hawahya?" Quinn felt like she'd landed on another planet.

Her family hadn't moved to Gulls Head, Massachusetts, for her, although the suckfest that was eighth grade would have been reason enough. They'd moved because of Quinn's nine-year-old brother, Julius. Because the Boulder public schools hadn't been "equipped" to meet his "special needs." (This was code for Julius had a lot of tantrums, banged his face against a few walls, bit the lunch lady.) Sometimes Quinn's brother did things and you had no idea why. Were the lights too bright in the cafeteria? Were the kids too loud? Did the lunch lady say something that made him want to bite her?

Julius's new school, the Cove, was supposed to be different. According to Quinn's mom, who had done all the research

7

and filled out the paperwork, the Cove was internationally renowned. It called itself a therapeutic day school for exceptional children, which was Julius, no doubt. Exceptional.

You could tell just by looking at his breakfast, which he was eating right now at the kitchen table. Wonder bread and cream cheese. Yogurt. Hardboiled egg, no yolk. Because today was Wednesday, and Julius ate only white foods on Wednesdays. Mondays he ate only meat. Fridays he ate only foods that were fried. This was the first thing you learned about Quinn's brother: he did things his own way. Throw off his system and you would witness destruction like you had never seen.

"White Wednesday," Julius said, lining up his utensils like train cars. "Right, Mo?" This was what he called their mom: Mo. Her real name was Maureen. That was another thing about Quinn's brother: he had his own way of speaking. For the first four years of his life, he hadn't spoken at all. Everyone was afraid he never would. Then one day, out of nowhere, he opened his mouth, and *bam!* Their dad was "Phil," Quinn was "Q," and Mom was "Mo." Once Julius started talking, he was a faucet you couldn't turn off. Sometimes it was long streams of words, sometimes it was short spurts.

"Right, Mo? White Wednesday. Right, Mo? Right?"

"That's right, buddy," Mo said, placing a glass of white milk on the table. There was brown under her fingernails. Clay. Quinn's mom was a sculptor. Heads and busts, mostly. When they'd lived in Boulder her pieces had sold in galleries

8

downtown, but Gulls Head didn't have much of an art scene, so Quinn didn't know how it was going to work out for her mom here. Quinn didn't know how it was going to work out for any of them. Her dad had taken an adjunct professorship. They were only renting this house. Flying by the seat of their pants, that was what they were doing.

While Quinn was standing in the kitchen doorway thinking how crazy it was that her family had just picked up and moved two thousand miles for Julius to try a new school, her mom looked up from the box she was unpacking. "Morning, Q," she said. She was wearing an old flannel shirt of Quinn's dad's, ripped jeans, clogs. Her hair was in a messy bun, held in place with a pencil.

"Morning," Quinn said.

Her mom's eyes hovered on Guinevere. Quinn waited for her to comment, but she didn't. Even though this was the first time Mo had seen Quinn in a wig since she'd tried on about fifty of them at Belle's Wig Botik in Denver. Even though Quinn had been wearing the same ratty Colorado Rockies baseball cap every day for a year. Mo smiled, and her eyes crinkled at the corners. "Hungry?" she said.

Quinn's poor mom. She was trying so hard to act normal, like her daughter wasn't wearing a costume.

"A little," Quinn said.

"Hardboiled egg?" Mo gestured to a bowl on the table.

"Okay."

"The most hardboiled eggs to be peeled and eaten in a minute is six." Quinn's brother said this without looking up. His hair was a mess. Spiky all over like a blond stegosaurus.

"Morning, Julius." Quinn pulled out a chair.

"Ashrita Furman of the USA." He added a fork to his utensil train. "At the offices of the Songs of the Soul, in New York, New York, USA, on twenty-three March two thousand and twelve. Each egg was weighed and was more than fifty-eight grams. All eggs were peeled and consumed within one minute."

That was another thing Julius did. He repeated things. Not just stuff he'd heard, like lines from commercials or TV shows or movies, but whole passages from books he'd read. He didn't care if you were interested or not. He'd say it anyway.

"All eggs were peeled and consumed within one minute."

"Wow," Quinn said, taking an egg from the bowl.

"*Wow* is a palindrome."

"Yes, it is."

"A palindrome reads the same forward and backward."

"Yes, it does." Quinn cracked the egg on the table.

"The longest known palindromic word is *saippuakivikauppias*, which is Finnish for a dealer in lye."

"Cool," she said.

"*Cool* is not a palindrome."

"I know."

"*Cool* does not read the same forward and backward."

Shut up, Quinn sometimes wanted to whisper. But she never did.

. . . . .

"You don't have to drive me," Quinn said as she strapped herself into the front seat. "I can walk."

"I don't mind driving you," her mom said.

"I don't mind walking."

"It's your first day," Mo said. "I want to see you off."

Quinn shrugged, holding the basketball in her lap. It was a new one, barely scuffed. Her dad had bought it for her before they left Colorado. This basketball was her tabula rasa, her blank slate.

As the car backed out of the driveway, Julius began muttering to himself from the backseat, *Guinness World Records 2017* propped in his lap, bright yellow headphones clamped to his ears.

"So," Mo said, glancing over at Quinn. "Are you nervous?" They had the same eyes, hazel, that shifted from brown to gold to green depending on the light. Mood eyes, her mom called them.

"I'm okay," Quinn said. It wasn't exactly a lie. Even though her scalp itched and she worried that the five pieces of wig tape she'd used might not be enough. What if they didn't stick? What if Guinevere came flying off in the middle of PE?

"That skirt looks nice," her mom said.

It was denim with red stitching. Quinn felt stupid wearing it. She never wore skirts.

"Thanks," Quinn said. She should have worn shorts and her Colorado Rockies baseball cap. But no. *No.* That was the whole problem back in Boulder. Just thinking about eighth grade—her bald head, her mesh basketball shorts, long and loose around her knees—Quinn felt a small, sharp twinge of shame. *Mr. Clean. Vin Diesel.* "You're bringing this on yourself," Paige had said once. "Why don't you make an effort?"

Well, Quinn was making an effort now, wasn't she? The wig. The skirt. If she looked like all the other girls at Gulls Head High School, maybe she would blend in. She'd be one of those leaf-tailed geckos, mimicking the foliage of its habitat so no predators would eat it. This was Quinn's plan: avoid being eaten.

Snap, snap, snap.

She heard Julius start to snap his fingers. Slowly at first, then picking up speed. Her mom heard, too, and she glanced in the rearview mirror.

"Bud?" Mo said quietly. "You okay?" She always stayed calm, even when Quinn's brother began to lose it. They were like equal and opposite forces. The more he amped up, the mellower she became.

Julius mumbled something, still snapping away.

"What's that?" Mo said.

"Tea and cakes," Julius blurted out.

12

"Ah," Mo said.

Quinn didn't ask, as if not asking would defuse the situation.

"T and Cakes," her mom said anyway. "It's the bakery in Boulder. We used to stop on the way to his school."

"Tea and cakes, Mo. Tea and cakes."

"That's right, buddy. You miss those white-chocolate scones, don't you? They were part of our old Wednesday routine."

Quinn squeezed her basketball. She listened to her mom try to soothe Julius, but there was no soothing him. Now they were going to have to drive all over Gulls Head, Massachusetts, looking for white-chocolate scones. Quinn wished they didn't have to. She wished, just once, that a ride in the car could be just a ride and not an episode of *My Strange Addiction*. She wished so many things. She wished that her brother's brain could be rewired. She wished that their entire lives did not revolve around his food. She wished that her dad didn't have to get up at five a.m. to take the commuter rail to work instead of riding his bike the way he had in Boulder. She wished that she still had hair. Even though she had never been one of those girly girls like Paige and Tara, who worried about clothes and nail polish and bad hair days, now that it was gone she missed it. She really did.

It had started last summer, a week before Quinn's thirteenth birthday. They'd been in the pool in their backyard when Julius had said, "Hair, Q. Hair." Before Quinn could

13

ask what he was talking about, her brother had launched into one of his monologues. "Xie Qiuping from China has been growing her hair since nineteen seventy-three. She now holds the record for the longest female hair with a length of five-point-six-two-seven meters when last measured. That's nearly as long as the height of a giraffe. Susa Forster from Breitenfelde, Germany, has two thousand four hundred and seventy-three giraffe items that she has collected . . ."

Julius had droned on until Quinn tuned him out and continued practicing her back dive. But that night, when she was getting ready for bed, she'd looked in the mirror and seen what her brother had been talking about: a bald patch about the size of a quarter, right near her part. It was probably nothing, she thought. Maybe she'd been wearing her ponytail too tight. Then she showed her mom, and Mo found two more spots—one at the back of Quinn's head, the other above her left ear. Mo told her not to worry. Maybe Quinn had a vitamin deficiency. Maybe it was hormones. Still, Mo called Dr. Steiner first thing the next morning. Dr. Steiner sent them to another doctor, a dermatologist named Dr. Hersh, who stuck Quinn's head under a light and peered at her scalp through magnifying glasses. He took off his glasses and spoke: "Alopecia areata." The words sounded like some food Quinn had never tasted but already knew she would hate. Baba ghanoush. Ratatouille.

"It's an autoimmune disorder," he said. "Your white blood cells are attacking your hair follicles."

"The hair could grow back," he said, "or it could fall out completely. We'll just have to wait and see."

Quinn's mom had squeezed Quinn's hand. She'd said they would go get ice cream. Chocolate chip and butter pecan. Hot fudge. Whipped cream. Nuts, sprinkles, the works. They had eaten like goddesses. Then they had driven home and watched Quinn's hair fall out.

Paige and Tara had watched, too. Every few days that summer, another spot would appear, until finally, by the second week of eighth grade, there was nothing left. Paige and Tara pretended not to care. They knew it wasn't Quinn's fault. They knew she wasn't contagious. But still, Quinn felt a distance growing between them. She felt a gaping hole of loss.

Wasn't it weird to miss something you'd never thought twice about? And here was another weird but true thing: Quinn was glad her family had moved, even if they'd done it for Julius. Because no one in Gulls Head, Massachusetts, knew that Guinevere wasn't her real hair. No one knew about her brother, either.

"Tea and cakes!"

She could be anyone.

"Tea and cakes! Tea and cakes!"

Anyone at all.

"Eee, eee, eee!"

Julius was starting to shriek and smack his head with the flat of his palm. Next would come the book.

"Buddy," Mo said quietly. "Gentle hands."

15

"Mom," Quinn said.

"Gentle, Julius. We will find you a scone as soon as we drop off your sister."

"Eee, eee, eee!"

You never knew what would set Julius off. It could be a hundred different things. Transitions. Noise. Hunger. Fatigue. Whatever the reason, when he got like this, it took forever to calm him down.

"*Mom*," Quinn said louder. "Pull over. I'll walk."

Mo sighed. "Q, please . . . It's your first day. I want to bring you."

"You can bring me tomorrow." The thought of arriving at Gulls Head High School with her brother hitting himself and screaming "tea and cakes" from the backseat was more than Quinn could bear. She reached down and grabbed her backpack. "Just let me out here, okay? I know where I'm going."

Quinn did know. All week she had been riding around on her skateboard, exploring, looking for a decent court.

"Eee, eee, eee!"

Here came the book.

"Julius," Mo said, dead calm. "Stop." She was pulling over, not to let Quinn out, but to remove *Guinness World Records 2017* from her brother's hands before he broke his own nose. He'd done that before. Twice.

"Honey, wait," Mo said, climbing into the backseat. "Just give us a minute."

But Quinn was already opening the door. Outside, the air

smelled briny and sharp. She took a good, deep swallow, filling her lungs. "I'll see you later, Mom."

"Are you sure?" Mo was wrestling the book from Julius's grip.

"I'm sure," Quinn said.

Even though she wished she were wearing sneakers instead of these stupid wedge sandals that she'd only worn once to her cousin Nadine's wedding, and even though she would probably get blisters, it felt good to walk away.

CHAPTER
2

QUINN WAS TRYING TO BLEND in with her new habitat, but Mr. Kellar's homeroom had assigned seats, and her desk was dead center. All through attendance she could feel the eyeballs on her. It was mostly sideways glances, no outright stares, but still. The feeling of so many eyeballs made the skin on Quinn's neck prickle. It made her want to reach up and pat Guinevere, just to be sure. Were five pieces of wig tape enough? What if she started to sweat? Quinn willed her hands to stay down. She focused her attention on the #2 pencil in front of her. Its smooth yellow coating. Its perfectly pink, never-before-used eraser.

Tabula rasa, Quinn thought. *Blank slate.*

Back in Colorado, there had been a dry-erase board on the wall in Quinn's kitchen. Every morning, before her dad left for work, he would write some random Latin phrase on the board for Quinn to contemplate. *Carpe diem. Ex nihilo nihil fit. Vincit qui se vincit.*

When Mr. Kellar began walking around the room, handing out schedules, Quinn slipped her phone out of her pocket and texted her dad:

Never got my quote this AM.

Fortes fortuna adiuvat, her dad texted back. Fortune favors the brave.

It was his first day of school, too. He was the adjunct professor of classics at some college Quinn had never heard of. She wondered if he missed UC Boulder. She wondered if he was nervous. She pictured her sweet, dorky dad, standing alone at the front of some lecture hall, holding a stub of chalk, clearing his throat.

"McAvoy?"

Quinn looked up. Mr. Kellar's face was as round and white as the moon.

"Yuh schedule. Put it in yuh bindah."

He might as well be speaking Latin.

. . . . .

First-period PE. Ten laps around the gym. If this were 408 days ago, Quinn would not have minded. She was born to run.

19

Quinn's mom loved to tell this story, about the first day she brought Quinn to diaper dance class at the parks and recreation center. Quinn was two years old. Paige and Tara were two years old, too. That was how they all met, in the multipurpose room at parks and rec, the three moms with their Starbucks cups, the three girls in their tutus and ballet slippers. Except Quinn had wanted nothing to do with ballet. As soon as she walked in the door, she spotted one of those rubber playground balls, stripped off her leotard, and began tearing around the room, bouncing the ball. Paige and Tara had thought Quinn was hilarious. They'd stripped off their leotards, too, and started running after her.

In first-period PE at Gulls Head High School, Quinn was the opposite of her two-year-old self. She was trying *not* to stand out. She was trying to keep everything *on*. Nice and easy. Slow jog. No sudden movements.

So far, the wig tape was holding. So far, no one had called Quinn a freak, or an alien, or, her personal favorite, "penis head."

The girls running laps behind her were talking rapid fire. "Oh my gawd, did you see Nick at Ivy's lockah? He was totally waiting for her."

"That is, like, so sad. Is he still texting her twenty times a day?"

"More like fifty."

"My cousin Angela? When she broke up with her

boyfriend? He wouldn't take no for an answer and he kept, like, texting and calling and showing up at her house? She had to get a restraining ordah."

"Oh my gawd, are you serious? Do you think he'll, like— Ivy! Ivy, oh my gawd, did you see your stawkah? He's back."

Apparently, Ivy had arrived.

"Don't call him a stawkah," Quinn heard her say. Then, "I feel bad. I've been avoiding him."

Immediately they jumped to her defense. "Don't feel bad. You broke up forever ago."

"You don't owe him anything. You brought him, like, fifty care packages this summah."

"It's not your fault he can't move on."

"I heard he could totally be walking by now but it's, like, all mental."

"Wait—*walk* walk? On his hands?"

"No, dummy, on fake legs. They're called prosthetics."

"Like that surfah who got shark attacked?"

"That was her arm, not her legs. Bethany Hamilton."

"Wasn't she in that movie?"

Soul Surfer, Quinn thought but did not say. She knew better than to join the conversation. She knew, without even turning around, what kind of girls they were. She could tell by their *oh my gawd*s. In the hallway, she could tell by the way they tossed their hair over their bare, tanned shoulders, by the way their lip gloss shimmered in the light. Even though Quinn had never cared about being popular—had always found Paige and Tara's obsession with coolness seriously weird—when one of the girls jogged up beside her, Quinn's chin automatically lifted, her stride lengthened.

"Hawahya?" the girl said. She was wearing a blue tank top. She was small and golden skinned with brown, curly hair gathered on top of her head in a big bouquet.

"Fine," Quinn said.

"You're new, right?" She was at least five inches shorter than Quinn, but she matched Quinn's pace.

"Yeah," Quinn said.

"Ivy D'Arcy." She held out one tanned hand with fuchsia fingernails and a bunch of silver rings.

"Quinn McAvoy," Quinn said, taking it, even though shaking hands sideways felt like they were running a relay and she was receiving the baton.

"Quinn," Ivy repeated.

"It's my mom's maiden name. Weird, I know, but it could be worse. My brother was named after the drink she craved the whole time she was pregnant."

"Really?"

"Yup. Orange Julius."

"Your brothah's name is *Orange Julius*?"

"Thankfully, no. Just Julius."

"Oh." Ivy snort-laughed. "I was gonna say."

"Yeah."

"Youngah or oldah?"

"Younger. He just turned nine."

Quinn passed under one of the basketball hoops, wishing she could stop and shoot a hundred free throws. She didn't want to talk about her brother. Trying to explain Julius was like trying to describe color to a blind person. Paige and Tara understood. They'd known Julius since he was born. But Quinn had seen enough strangers stare at her brother in public. Most people had heard of autism spectrum disorder, but very few had seen a kid like Julius in action. Quinn could already picture Ivy's face closing up, her polite nod taking over.

"Hey." Another girl appeared on Ivy's left. Long black hair, red lips, crop top and short-shorts. "I'm Cahmen."

Cahmen? Carmen. Right.

"I'm Lissa." A third girl materialized. Stick thin with silver leggings and corn-silk hair.

"This is Quinn," Ivy said. "The one all the boys are talking about."

Quinn squared her shoulders, waiting for the punch line. In Boulder, the boys had been even worse than the girls. *Quinn's so bald you can rub her head and see the future. Quinn's so bald Mr. Clean is jealous.* After a while, Quinn had learned to ignore them. She'd learned to make her face completely blank, like a Botoxed celebrity, as though nothing they said could penetrate. This was a skill Quinn called upon now. Her face was prepared for anything.

"You're pretty," Ivy said, squinting up at Quinn. "Isn't she, girls?"

"For real," Carmen said. "You have the nicest hair."

Quinn almost tripped over her own feet.

Lissa said, "Is it natural?"

The spit in Quinn's mouth had formed a paste so thick she wasn't sure she could answer. But somehow she did. "Yes," she said, which was not exactly a lie. Estetica human hair wigs came from real, natural, human heads.

"Couldn't you just kill her?" Ivy said, but she was smiling, touching Quinn's arm like they'd been friends forever.

Across the gym, a whistle blasted. The gym teacher, a huge, mustached man in shorts so tight they looked painted on, hollered, "All right, people, circle up!"

. . . . . .

Between first-period PE and fifth-period lunch, Quinn met three Emmas, two Avas, a Kacey, a Kylie, a Kelsie, and a Chelsey. She met a Jack, a Zach, a Mason, a Carson, a Tyler, and a Darius. She met a Mr. Fenner, a Ms. Chin, a Mrs. Wengender, and a Mrs. Winternitz. Every time someone told Quinn their name, she forgot it. There were so many faces. Everyone talked so fast. "Nice to meet you," she said, over and over. And "Boulder, Colorado." And "Yeah, it's really nice here."

In fourth-period art, over a tin of shared watercolors, one of the Emmas said to Quinn, "You must feel like a movie stah."

24

"A movie star?" Quinn shook her head, embarrassed. "Why?"

"Because you're new. And nothing new evah happens in Gulls Head. It's, like, the most boring town on the planet."

. . . . .

As soon as Quinn walked into freshman lunch, there were the girls from PE: Ivy, Carmen, and Lissa.

"Come on," Ivy said. She literally grabbed Quinn by the arm and pulled her across the room. "You're sitting with us."

So now, here she was, sitting at a table with Ivy, Carmen, and Lissa, unwrapping her peanut butter and honey sandwich and answering more questions. Where did she live in Gulls Head? What kind of music did she like? Did she cheerlead? Did she play field hockey? Was that the new iPhone? It was wicked cool.

Wicked. They liked that word a lot.

They also liked lip gloss.

"Balmy Weathah," Carmen said when Lissa asked what kind she was wearing.

"Bikini or Sangria?"

"Bikini," Carmen said, slicking some onto her lips with her little wand.

"Balmy is the bomb," Ivy said.

"Balmy is the bomb," they all agreed.

Quinn took a bite of her sandwich and said nothing. Because she had nothing to add. The glossiest thing she had ever put on her lips was ChapStick. If Julius were here, he would launch right in with one of his records. *The most lipstick applications in one hour is five hundred and thirty-five.* Thankfully, Julius was not here. Thankfully, no one at the table seemed to notice Quinn's makeup deficiency. They were more interested in where she'd bought her skirt (Buffalo Exchange) and whether or not she had a boyfriend back in Colorado (not). Which brought them full circle to the conversation Quinn had overheard while running laps.

"You see that boy ovah by the window?" Ivy whispered. "In the wheelchair?"

Quinn turned around.

"Don't *look*," Lissa said.

Quinn turned back to her sandwich.

"That's my ex-boyfriend," Ivy said.

His name, Quinn was told in hushed tones, was Nick Strout. Brother of Tommy Strout, junior, quarterback of the varsity football team. There were two more Strout brothers who'd graduated. Football royalty, all of them. Tommy Strout was the most gorgeous specimen of all. Nick Strout, on the other hand, was a real-life tragedy.

"Why?" Quinn said.

"Because," Ivy said solemnly, "he was the best football playah Gulls Head has evah seen. Even in eighth grade."

"And now he has no legs," Lissa whispered.

"Gone." Carmen snapped her fingers. "Just like that."

Sitting there in the cafeteria, Quinn felt every cell in her body standing at attention. She remembered Dr. Hersh's words: *The hair could grow back, or it could fall out completely. We'll just have to wait and see.* She turned to Ivy and said, "What happened?"

"Snowmobile accident. Rollovah. He got crushed."

"Crushed," Lissa repeated.

"He almost died," Ivy said.

Carmen pointed her finger at the ceiling and held it there.

"Don't mind her," Ivy said.

"What is she doing?" Quinn said.

"Pointing up at God," Lissa said. "Like Big Papi."

"Who's Big Papi?"

Everyone stared at Quinn.

"You've nevah heard of Big Papi?" Carmen said.

Quinn shook her head, feeling stupider by the second.

"He's only the best baseball playah evah."

"Evah."

"You *have* heard of the Red Sox, haven't you?" Lissa said.

"Yes," Quinn said. "I've heard of the Red Sox." Did they think she was born under a rock?

"Anyway," Ivy said. "Nick was my boyfriend. But now he's not."

"Now he's her stawkah," Lissa said.

"He is not my *stawkah*," Ivy said. "He's just having trouble moving on."

By the time the bell rang, Quinn had learned two things about Nick Strout and Ivy D'Arcy:

1) They'd gone out for four months, three months before and one month after the snowmobile accident that crushed his legs.

2) Ivy dumped Nick not because an infection forced doctors to amputate Nick's legs, but because Nick (who used to be fun and cute and crazy talented) seemed to have undergone a personality amputation. Which was way worse than losing his legs. Now he was bitter and needy and, well, not the Nick Strout that Ivy had once loved. Like, at all.

This was what Quinn was contemplating on her way to sixth-period study hall: Nick Strout's chopped-off personality. You could probably call it ironic that the first person Quinn saw when she got to room 203 was Nick Strout. Unless this was some other boy in a wheelchair stuck on the door-jamb.

Quinn didn't *decide* to help him. It was instinct. She just bent down and tried to unwedge his wheel.

"What are you doing?"

Dark hair, dark eyes, ticked-off expression.

"Sorry," Quinn said when she realized she was staring. He had no legs. Well, he had legs. They just stopped at midthigh, poking out of his khaki shorts and covered in these white stocking things. "I didn't mean . . . I was just trying to . . ."

"What?" he snapped.

"I . . ."

"Do you have a staring problem?"

Quinn shook her head. She knew what it felt like to be stared at. She knew better than anyone. It started with a warm tingle in your cheeks that spread like gangrene down your neck and chest, and into your belly, where it took up residence, growing hotter and hotter, until your whole body was smoldering. She'd felt it all the time last year. At restaurants. At the grocery store. In line for the movies. *What's wrong with that girl? Why doesn't she have hair?*

Quinn wanted to tell Nick that she understood. But she couldn't. He was looking at her like . . . if he were holding a pencil he would stab her in the stomach. But he wasn't holding a pencil. Neither of them was. Because Quinn's pencil had dropped out of her hand and rolled under the wheelchair, and all she could do was stand there, stammering like an idiot. "Sorry . . . I didn't mean . . . I guess I'll just . . ." Her voice trailed off and she bent down to retrieve her pencil.

"Yo, Nicky!"

From her crouched position, Quinn turned her head. There was another boy down the hall. He had the same dark hair as Nick, but he was older and thicker looking, wearing a football jersey and holding up a cell phone.

"What?" Nick said.

"Mom's been texting you. Did you forget your phone again?"

29

Tommy Strout, Quinn thought. *Junior.*

Nick said nothing.

"You have a PT appointment at twelve thirty. She says she'll meet you out front."

Tommy Strout, Quinn thought. *Quarterback of the football team.*

The bell rang. She had no choice but to scramble up from her awkward position, clutching her pencil.

"Hey there," Tommy Strout said.

"Hey," Quinn said.

He smiled, slow and sweet and lopsided. It was the kind of smile that weakened knees and stopped hearts. And it would not be happening to Quinn McAvoy of Boulder, Colorado, she could promise you that. Despite the fact that she had fairly nice legs, which she was pretty sure he had noticed. In Boulder, all anyone had noticed was her head.

Gleam-o.

Baldilocks.

Shaquille O'Neal.

Quinn had half a mind to rip Guinevere off, kick her wedge sandals into the air, and yell, *April Fools!* But she didn't. She was Quinn McAvoy of Gulls Head, Massachusetts, and she was going to make a dignified exit into study hall. As dignified an exit as a girl could make in platform heels and a wig that might or might not be sliding off.

Quinn considered apologizing again, but Nick Strout wouldn't even look at her. He was shooting his death stare at the floor. And anyway, she had already apologized twice. Quinn McAvoy of Boulder, Colorado, would apologize three times. She would chastise herself and feel like crap for the rest of the day.

But Quinn was not that girl.

Not anymore.

CHAPTER

QUINN WAS HAPPY TO SEE HER MOM'S car pulling into the pickup line because it meant that she was just seconds away from taking off her shoes. Quinn's feet were dying. Her scalp was itching like mad, too. She would give it a good, long scratch if Ivy, Carmen, and Lissa weren't clumped around her in front of the school, firing questions. What did she think of her first day? Was she glad she'd moved here? Did she think any of the boys were cute?

It was exhausting. Not that Quinn was complaining about the attention. She wasn't. It was just that all this smiling and head bobbing was new to her. Not to mention being on high alert in case her skirt rose up or Guinevere decided to melt off her head in the heat of the day.

"Hi, honey," Quinn's mom said when Quinn finally got in the car.

"Hi." Quinn yanked off both sandals and sighed. Relief.
"How was it?"

"Good," Quinn said. Because she couldn't risk scratching
her scalp yet, she examined her feet. One, two, three . . . five
blisters.

"Good." Mo squeezed Quinn's arm as they pulled away
from the curb. She looked tired. More tired than she had that
morning, which was saying something. It probably meant
she'd been fielding calls from Julius's school all day. But Quinn
didn't ask. Having Mo to herself was a rare thing.

"Looks like you made some friends."

Quinn glanced in the side-view mirror at Ivy, Carmen, and
Lissa shrinking into the distance, attending to their tiny
phones.

"Yeah," she said, sounding surer than she felt. After the
suckfest that was eighth grade, Quinn was not as trusting as
she used to be. She could count on three fingers the number
of people she actually trusted now: 1) her mom, 2) her dad,
3) her grandma Gigi in Arizona. And Quinn had never told
any of them about Paige and Tara drifting away, or about the
names she'd been called, or about that One Stupid Night.

That One Stupid Night had taken place the Saturday before Valentine's Day, in Paige's basement. Paige, Tara, and
Quinn had been planning the party together for weeks.
They'd decorated Paige's basement (white Chinese lanterns,
heart-shaped balloons, confetti on the tables). They'd baked
(red velvet cupcakes, heart-shaped cookies). They'd made a

Valentine's playlist. They'd even worn matching outfits: hot-pink tights that they had bought at Target and oversized white T-shirts that they had graffitied with fabric markers. Candy heart messages like *Be Mine* and *Text Me* and *Crazy 4 U*. At Paige and Tara's request, Quinn hadn't worn the Colorado Rockies cap that night. She'd found a red-and-white-striped beanie with earflaps in the bargain bin at Anthropologie. It made her feel like a fighter pilot.

Paige's parents had been cool about the party. They'd greeted each guest at the door, but after that, they'd promised to stay upstairs and let the kids have fun.

For a while, fun had been the girls sitting on couches and the boys cramming mini cupcakes into one another's mouths. Then fun had been the girls dancing and the boys sucking helium out of the balloons and squeaking to one another like chipmunks. Finally, fun was Seven Minutes in Heaven.

Until that night, Quinn had never heard of Seven Minutes in Heaven, let alone played it. The idea had come from Sammy Albee, who was the youngest of six and seemed to know everything there was to know about boy-girl parties.

Quinn remembered Sammy Albee grinning as she held up a stack of paper strips in her fist. "Everyone write your name on one of these. Boys' names in the silver bucket. Girls' names in the white bucket."

Quinn had done as Sammy asked, just as everyone had done as Sammy asked. Sammy had that kind of personality. And even though there were very few eighth-grade boys

Quinn would have considered making out with for seven minutes in Paige's basement bathroom, she'd figured that whoever she got matched with, a girl's first kiss was a rite of passage. Quinn was almost fourteen. And this was, after all, a Valentine's party.

She'd stood there, drinking Hi-C, as names were called and couples filed in and out of the bathroom. Adrienne and Tyler. Kelly and Ben. Paige and Henry. There was giggling and hooting and blushing and a few dramatic gagging noises. And then, all of a sudden, the coolest thing happened.

"Quinn," Sammy said, reading a slip of paper from the silver bucket. "And"—Sammy stuck her hand into the white bucket—"Ethan."

Quinn and Ethan.

Actually, this was the worst possible thing that could have happened, but Quinn hadn't known it then. All she'd known was that Ethan Hess was the cutest boy in eighth grade, and if she had been able to pick anyone to play Seven Minutes in Heaven with, it would have been him.

It might have been Quinn's imagination, but when she and Ethan walked into the bathroom, the hooting and hollering was louder for them than it had been for any other couple. Quinn hadn't been thinking about her hair then. She knew she was bald. She knew Ethan knew she was bald. Her baldness had just seemed, in that moment, irrelevant. She felt cute in her fighter pilot beanie. And anyway, the lights were off.

"Hey," Ethan said in the dark.

"Hey," Quinn said back.

Ethan was taller than most of the eighth-grade boys. He looked older, too. He had real muscles under his T-shirt. Quinn had noticed on their way into the bathroom how his sleeves were tight and she could see the line of his deltoids right through the fabric. Standing in there with the door shut, she could smell his boy scent. Soap and grass and an undercurrent of sweat that wasn't exactly gross. Ethan Hess smelled like a basketball player, and Quinn knew he was good because the boys' team and the girls' team shared a court, and she had watched him scrimmage.

"So," Ethan said, taking a step closer. He was chewing cinnamon gum, which happened to be Quinn's favorite flavor.

"So," she said.

They'd both laughed a little, because it was weird to be standing in the dark in Paige's bathroom while everyone waited outside. Even though it was pitch-black, Quinn could picture the seashell wallpaper and the little starfish soaps that she'd washed her hands with a million times.

"Think you'll go all the way?" Ethan said.

"What?"

"Your team. You're in the quarterfinals, right?"

"Oh. Yeah." She had thought they would be kissing by then, but there they were, talking about basketball. "We'll make it to the semis at least."

"Yeah," he said. "Us too. Summit will be tough, but we can beat them."

Quinn registered every word Ethan was saying: Summit's shooting guard was tall, but he was a one-armed bandit. If they pushed him to the left, he had nothing. Against Casey Middle, they'd have to play the zone. But all she could really think about was the smell of his cinnamon gum and how, if she leaned in just a little, their lips would touch.

"Two minutes!" someone yelled from outside.

Had five minutes passed already? That's what Quinn was wondering when Ethan reached out and grabbed her boob right through her shirt.

"What are you doing?" she said.

She had been surprised more than anything else. Why would he do that? Had it been an accident? She remembered what she did next: she removed his hand from her boob and told him to keep his paws to himself. But then he did something even weirder: he grabbed *her* hand and put it between his legs, where the zipper of his jeans had already been unzipped.

Quinn remembered leaping back the same way she had in the haunted house on Halloween, when she'd stuck her hand in a bowl of eyeballs and intestines. Even though she knew they were really just peeled grapes and cold spaghetti, the feel of them had made her jump.

"Come on," Ethan pleaded. "We've only got two minutes."

"I don't care if we've got two years," Quinn said.

"Finish up, lovebirds!" a voice called from outside.

"No one has to know," Ethan said.

"No one is going to know," Quinn said, "because nothing is happening." She reached through the dark for the doorknob, but she wasn't fast enough. She felt the hat come off her head. "What are you doing? Give me that!" Her hands scrambled through the air, but she felt nothing.

That was when the door flew open. The lights came on. Ethan walked out of the bathroom with Quinn's hat dangling from his finger, smirking. "Gives new meaning to the word *head*."

Those were the words that would change everything. *Gives new meaning to the word head*. Quinn hadn't understood them at the time. She'd had no clue. All she knew when she walked out of Paige's bathroom was that Ethan Hess had her hat, and everyone was laughing, and she needed it back. She got it no problem. Ethan was so busy being high-fived and fist-bumped and back-slapped, he didn't care about the hat anymore. She grabbed it straight out of his hand and jammed it back on her head.

"What a jerk," she said to Paige and Tara when she managed to get them alone in a corner. "You won't believe what happened in there."

"We heard," Paige said. "Ethan's telling everyone."

"What?" Quinn said.

Tara's lip curled up the way it did when she was grossed out. "Please tell me you didn't *actually* give him head."

"I don't know even what that means," Quinn said.

"Sure you do."

"No. I don't."

"Oral," Paige said, leaning in and lowering her voice. "You know . . . *down there*. Not your hand, but your mouth."

"What?" Quinn remembered laughing at the thought. "That's disgusting. I would never do something like that."

"Ethan said you did."

"Well, I didn't."

"Well," Paige said finally, "good."

"Because that would be revolting," Tara said.

"I *know*," Quinn said.

"And really, really bad for your reputation," Paige said.

"Seriously," Tara said. "We're almost in high school, Quinn. You need to think about these things."

Quinn didn't like the way her friends were talking to her, like she was a little kid and they were her parents. But that wasn't even the worst part. The worst part was Sammy Albee walking over, grinning like a wolf. "Ethan's fly was down. Everyone saw."

"So?" Quinn said.

"So. Everyone knows what you did."

"I didn't do anything. We never even kissed."

The basement, Quinn suddenly realized, was silent. Someone had turned off the music. Everyone was looking at her.

She remembered exactly what happened next. She turned and looked straight at Ethan, who was standing over by the snack table, eating a heart-shaped cookie. A heart-shaped cookie that Quinn herself had baked.

"Tell them," she said. Her voice was loud and clear, but her chest was tight. "Tell them nothing happened in the bathroom." She wondered how Ethan could be eating a cookie right now. If she had tried to put anything in her mouth, she would have barfed.

"Ha," Ethan said, spraying crumbs through the air when he spoke. "Good one, Gandhi."

"My name," she said, still loud, but now her voice was shaking, "is *Quinn*. And *nothing* happened in that bathroom."

But it hadn't mattered that she was telling the truth. It hadn't mattered that Paige and Tara believed her. Because no one else at the party did. Neither did any of the eighth-grade girls on Quinn's basketball team, who hadn't even been at Paige's house, but who, before practice on Monday, confronted Quinn in the locker room to let her know that they'd heard about her "slutty behavior" on Saturday night and that it "didn't reflect well on the team."

Nothing was the same after that. Nothing.

Paige and Tara hadn't stopped being her friends, exactly. They were too nice for that. The changes were subtle. Like Quinn would text them and they would take a little longer to text back. Or they would start "running late" for school so they had to get rides, and Quinn would walk to school on her own. Then there were the comments. *You're bringing this on yourself, Quinn. If you don't want people to call you names, why don't you make an effort? Wear a pretty scarf. Stop coming to school all sweaty.*

Once or twice, Mo mentioned something. "I haven't seen Paige or Tara in a while. Is everything okay?"

"Sure," Quinn would say. "Everything's fine."

Because here was the thing: unless you had a brother like Julius, you wouldn't understand. If Quinn were to come home from school and say, "Hey, Mom and Dad, can I talk to you?" they would say, "Of course. Just let us get Julius settled." That was another thing that sounded simple but wasn't. Julius needed his snack arranged on a tray. He required three different foods, all of which had to meet the day-of-the-week criteria, and none of which could touch. The seams of his socks had to be straight at all times. He needed three blankets when he was watching TV, and they could not be wrinkled. Not only was the process of settling Quinn's brother torturously slow, but if anyone deviated from the plan, the meltdown that followed could be epic. Julius didn't care who saw. He didn't care who got hurt. When he lost it, he lost it completely. Lamps flew. Bystanders got kicked, punched, scratched. One time, he melted down in the grocery store, and afterward, the cereal aisle looked like a war zone. Quinn felt so bad that her mom and dad had to deal with Julius that the last thing she wanted was to unload on them.

"Preternaturally self-sufficient." Those were the words Quinn's mom had used to describe her once, on the phone with Grandma Gigi. Quinn remembered because she'd had to look up the word *preternatural*. Grandma Gigi was a retired social worker and a great listener, but she had been diagnosed with Alzheimer's last year, so it wasn't like Quinn was going to call her up and say, *Hey, Geege, let me tell you about all the bad stuff that's been happening to me.*

"Q," her mom said.

"Huh?" Quinn was staring out the window as they passed by the Gulls Head High School athletic fields.

"I asked if you were itchy today."

"A little," Quinn said. Now that she was out of eyesight, she could finally lift Guinevere and scratch. And scratch. And scratch some more.

"Did you try the witch hazel?"

This was one of the tips they had received from the perky blond wig technician at Belle's Wig Botik in Denver: *If you're going to wear a wig all day, put a few drops of witch hazel on a damp cloth and wipe it over your scalp once every two to three hours.*

Right. Like Quinn would ever ask for a bathroom pass in the middle of geometry. *Pardon me while I zip to the girls' room and witch-hazel my head.*

"I'll try it when we get home," Quinn said.

Mo glanced at her watch. "I need to pick Julius up at four. We have a meeting with his therapy team at four fifteen."

"Can you just drop me at the house?" Quinn said, because the last place she wanted to go was her brother's therapy team meeting.

"It takes twenty minutes to get to the Cove. I don't want to be late."

"Please?"

Mo glanced at her watch again, then at Quinn.

"I've got homework," Quinn said.

"Already?"

"Yes." It was easier than saying how much she did not want to go to Julius's school or how badly she needed to take off this wig. She knew Mo meant well, but Quinn really didn't need any more itchy-scalp advice from someone with hair. "I need the computer," she added, in case her mom was about to tell her that she could do her homework in the car.

It worked.

The minute Mo dropped her off at the house, Quinn unlocked the front door, ripped Guinevere off, and flung her into the living room. She gave her scalp a good, long scratch. Then she remembered that this one stupid wig had cost her parents two thousand bucks. God, what a racket—but Quinn felt bad, so she put Guinevere upstairs, back on the Styrofoam head where she belonged, so she wouldn't lose her shape.

Now Quinn was bald and barefoot in front of the iMac in her dad's makeshift office, free to log in to her chat room. Quinn's username was FuzzyWuzzy. As in "Fuzzy Wuzzy was a bear, Fuzzy Wuzzy had no hair, Fuzzy Wuzzy wasn't fuzzy, was he?" There was a certain amount of sick humor on alopeciasucks.com.

She began to type.

Day one with a wig. Reason: new school. Outcome: mixed. Pros: 1) "hair" was a big hit, even got

complimented, 2) not being called Gandhi. Cons:
1) worried all day that wig tape wouldn't hold, 2) so
freaking hot and itchy, like fire ants eating my scalp.
Does this mean I will go qball tomorrow? Highly
doubtful. Just need to dunk my head in witch hazel
tonight, I guess (???). Verdict: fraudulence can be fun.

It didn't take long for the responses to roll in.

TheNewNormal: Way to go, Fuzz! Didn't u feel so
much better in public? I will never go back to
qballing.
T'sallGood: U r not a fraud, Fuzzy. U r just trying to
feel good about yourself. No harm in that.
BaldFacedTruth: Have u tried Oregon grape root?
It's a plant extract. There's this spritz u can use before
u put on your wig. "Oregon Conditioning Spray."
Highly recommend.
WigginOut: Or u can wear a wig liner . . .
HairlessWonder: Best wig tape for sensitive skin is
Walker brand 3M. They sell scalp protector too.
TheEyebrowsHaveIt: Are u AAU? If so I recommend
Cardani Human Hair Eyebrow Wigs #15. No itch,
and u can sleep with them on!

AAU stood for *alopecia areata universalis*. This was the
rarest type of alopecia areata, resulting in 100 percent

full-body hair loss, which meant eyebrows, eyelashes, pits, pubes, leg hair, everything. Not to be confused with AAP (alopecia areata patchy), where the hair on your head fell out in random spots, or AAT (alopecia areata totalis), which was what Quinn had. Even though she'd started out patchy, she had since lost every hair on her scalp but nowhere else. All things considered, Quinn was lucky. She couldn't imagine wearing eyebrow wigs.

Thanks, guys, she wrote. I'll let u know how it goes.

CHAPTER

QUINN'S MOM CAME BACK FROM HER MEETING at the Cove
with homework. Not for Julius, who was parked in front
of the TV with his three blankets, but for Quinn and her
dad, who were parked at the kitchen table with their ice
cream.

"Here's what we need to determine," Mo said. She held up
a sheet of paper and began reading. "'What are Julius's
strengths? Which of his behaviors are causing the most problems? How does he learn best? What does he enjoy and how
can those activities be used at home and school?'"

"Hmmm," Quinn said, pretending to contemplate these
questions while she helped herself to another scoop of Chunky
Monkey. "Guinness World Records. Guinness World Records. Guinness World Records. And . . . uhhh . . . Guinness
World Records."

"Q," Mo said.

"Am I wrong?"

Quinn gestured with her spoon toward the living room, where Julius was watching an old DVD of *Guinness World Records Primetime* that he'd seen so many times the whole family had it memorized.

"Does this man have the world's biggest mouth?" Quinn spoke into her spoon, making her voice deep and booming like the announcer's. *"It's Jim Purol versus one hundred fifty straws in a Guinness Record attempt that will make you gag!"*

"She has a point," Quinn's dad said, taking a bite of Chunky Monkey. *"Puer obsessi."*

"He is not *a boy obsessed*," Mo said. "He is a boy for whom routine is critically important. Guinness World Records are a part of his routine."

"Fair enough," Quinn's dad said. "But when does *routine*"— he paused to scratch quote marks in the air with his fingers— "become so limiting that a person can't enter the real world?"

Mo shook her head. "We've talked about this, Phil. The real world for Julius and the real world for us are two different things. The real world for Julius is a confusing mess of sounds and sights and people and places. He needs structure. Order. Predictability. When he opens up the same book every morning, he knows exactly what to expect. When he turns on the same DVD every night after dinner, he knows exactly what to expect."

"I understand," Quinn's dad said, "but are we doing him

47

a disservice by not teaching him other ways to cope? By not expanding his horizons?"

"Not expanding his horizons?" Mo's eyebrows shot up. "We just moved our son all the way across the country. We've altered his physical environment, his social environment, everything he has ever known. We've thrown him into chaos."

"Whose idea was that?" Quinn's dad said. Not unkindly. Quinn's dad was always kind.

"Believe me," Mo said, "if a school like the Cove existed in Boulder, we would still be in Boulder. But it doesn't. So we aren't. We are in Gulls Head, Massachusetts. And I would like for us to take advantage of the exceptional resources we now have at our disposal to help Julius."

"Fair enough," Quinn's dad said.

"Q?" Mo said. "Are you with us?"

"I'm with you."

Quinn's dad reached out, ruffled the top of Quinn's head. There was nothing there to ruffle, but his hand was warm.

"Okay," Mo said. "Let's try this again."

She held up the sheet of paper. "How can we provide a predictable routine for Julius that will incorporate his new house, new town, and new school?"

. . . . . .

At night, Quinn had her own routine. She would never tell anyone, not in a million years, but here it was:

First, she would turn out all the lights in her room. Next, she would sit on her bed in the dark, running her fingers over every square inch of her scalp, like a newly blind person trying to read braille. Were there any raised dots yet?

The next thing Quinn would do was sing. She knew it was stupid, which was why she would never tell anyone, but thinking about her bald head always made her think about the Frog and Toad story she'd loved when she was little, where Toad wants to grow a garden. He plants a bunch of flower seeds in his backyard. When they don't grow right away, he starts shouting at them. Frog tells Toad to leave the seeds alone, to let the sun and rain do their work, but Toad refuses to listen to logic. He tries everything he can think of to make the garden grow. He reads stories to his seeds. He plays music to his seeds. He sings to his seeds.

The song Quinn sang to her bald head was even stupider than the fact that she was singing at all. "Livin' on a Prayer" by Bon Jovi. Her dad would appreciate the song choice. Phil was a huge Bon Jovi fan. He was, in fact, the reason Quinn knew all the lyrics, not just to "Livin' on a Prayer," but to every song on the *Slippery When Wet* album. But her dad still wouldn't get why Quinn was singing to her bald head. No one would get it.

So she sang very softly. So softly she could barely hear herself.

"Tommy used to work on the docks."

CHAPTER

IN A WEIRD WAY, Quinn had Paige and Tara to thank for her basketball skills. In seventh grade she had been an okay-but-not-great shooting guard. In eighth grade, when Paige and Tara began "running late" in the mornings and needed to get rides, Quinn began walking to school alone. She would dribble her basketball—crossovers, in-and-outs, hesitations—stopping at Canyon Park to sink ten free throws before she would let herself move on.

Once Quinn got in the habit, she didn't want to stop. So here was what she planned to do on the second morning of her new life: dribble her new basketball to her new school, stopping at her new court to sink ten free throws before she would let herself move on.

This time, Mo didn't even argue about dropping Quinn off. Mo was too busy coaxing Julius into the car. She was using her new approach: positive reinforcement. Personally, Quinn thought it was insulting to her brother's intelligence to give him a smiley face sticker for putting on his seat belt, but she kept that opinion to herself. She was just happy to be gliding down the street on her skateboard, basketball in her hands, ten pieces of Walker brand 3M wig tape on her head.

Bounce, cross, bounce, cross, bounce, cross.

The salt air filled her lungs. Until two weeks ago, Quinn had never smelled this smell. She had never seen the ocean. The Colorado River, yes. The Blue Mesa Reservoir, yes. But never the ocean.

Now Gulls Head Beach was just a few blocks from Quinn's house. She'd found the court when she was out exploring. It was really just an extension of the beach parking lot. One hoop, nothing fancy, but with a great view of the water.

Quinn skidded to a stop on the sand. She checked her watch. Seven minutes to make ten free throws. No problem.

She left her skateboard and backpack on the ground and dribbled over to the foul line.

Bounce, bounce, catch. Bounce, bounce, catch.

One thing Quinn had learned from her coach back in Colorado was that every shooter has a different routine when she steps up to the foul line. Quinn's routine was two dribbles, hold. Two dribbles, hold. Then she would lift the ball in her right hand, make an L with her elbow, and lock her eyes on the rim.

As soon as she released the ball, Quinn knew someone was

51

watching. She felt that prickle on the back of her neck. After she made the shot she glanced over her shoulder and saw Nick Strout. He was maybe fifteen feet away, sitting in his wheelchair. Black shorts. Red shirt. Wet hair.

A crazy question popped into Quinn's head then. Not *Where did he come from?* but *How does he take a shower?* Did he use some kind of seat? Did his mom help him?

"Hi," Quinn said, because she certainly wasn't about to ask Nick Strout how he took a shower.

He didn't say anything, just looked at her.

"Do you live over there?" she asked, cocking her head at the row of houses across the street.

Nick didn't answer.

Quinn stood there, waiting for a response.

Nothing.

Fine. If he wasn't going to talk, she would keep shooting. Nine free throws to go.

Bounce, bounce, catch. Bounce, bounce, catch. Elbow. Eyes. Release. Swish.

Bounce, bounce, catch. Bounce, bounce, catch. Elbow. Eyes. Release. Swish.

Bounce, bounce, catch. Bounce, bounce, catch. Elbow. Eyes. Release. Swish.

"Nice shot!"

This time when Quinn turned around it wasn't Nick she saw, it was Tommy. Tommy Strout, junior, driving a car so ugly and beat-up Quinn almost laughed. There was rust every-where. There was duct tape holding up the fender.

"Yo, Nicky!" Tommy called out the window. "Mom said to come get you and take you to school."

"I don't need a babysitter," Nick said. He puffed out his chest, but his damp hair was curling up around his ears like wings, which, Quinn thought, ruined the tough-guy effect.

"I'm not your babysitter," Tommy said. "I'm your chauf-feur."

He didn't have the Boston accent, Quinn realized. He said his *R*s the way you were supposed to.

Nick muttered something Quinn didn't catch.

"You gonna introduce me or what?" Tommy said.

Nick ignored the question. He rolled his wheelchair around to the other side of the car.

No matter. Here was that smile coming at Quinn, slow and sweet and lopsided. Here was a hand, reaching out the window. "Hey. I'm Tom."

Quinn walked over, clutching the basketball to her hip. She was glad she wasn't wearing yesterday's sandals. She was wearing her Converse low-tops with a pair of semi-nice white shorts and a purple T-shirt with a scoop neck.

"Quinn," she said.

They shook hands.

"Nice to meet you, Quinn."

53

She nodded. Because his skin was warm and his grip was strong, and she was finding words difficult to come by.

"You play?" He jutted his chin at the basketball.

She nodded.

"Cool." Then, "You a freshman?"

She nodded again.

"Need a ride?"

"That's okay." Quinn's voice sounded almost normal, which she was glad about. She pointed to her skateboard, lying in the sand. "I've got a ride."

Tommy smiled. "Nice wheels."

"Thanks." She glanced through the window. More duct tape. Pink fuzzy dice hanging from the rearview. "You, too."

From the other side of the car Nick muttered something else.

"'Scuse me, Quinn," Tommy said. He opened the driver's side door.

As soon as she realized what was happening—Tommy was helping Nick out of his wheelchair and into the backseat—she averted her eyes. *Look away*, her brain said. *Don't stare*.

"I should go," she said, bending down to grab her skateboard. She'd only made four free throws, not ten, but she knew it was time.

"Nice meeting you, Quinn," Tommy said.

"You, too."

She didn't glance back once. When Tommy Strout's junk heap of a car passed her on the street, he honked and Quinn waved. Nick was staring straight ahead. His wheelchair was sticking half out of the trunk, like a loose tooth.

. . . . .

In PE, Ivy, Carmen, and Lissa were hunched together on a wrestling mat, looking at something.

"Quinn," Carmen said when she noticed Quinn leaning against the wall. "Check this out."

"What is it?" Quinn said.

"Tommy Strout," Ivy said, holding up her phone. "In the flesh."

Quinn walked over for a closer look. There was Tommy, all right, in the same shorts and muscle shirt he'd been wearing at the beach earlier, holding Nick's wheelchair in the air like a heavyweight champion.

"I took it this morning," Ivy said. "Right outside, when he was dropping Nick off."

"How nice is he, driving his brother to school?" Lissa said.

"So nice."

"Zoom in," Carmen said.

Ivy zoomed in on the screen, and the wheelchair disappeared. Now it was just Tommy from behind.

"Look at his arms," Lissa said softly. "He is so built."

"Forget his arms," Carmen said. "Look at his butt. You can see the outline right through his shorts."

"Ew," Lissa said.

"Why ew? He has a great gluteus maximus."

"He has a great everything," Ivy said. She cocked her head at Quinn. "Don't you think?"

"Sure," Quinn said. "Except for his car."

"What do you know about his cah?"

"He offered me a ride this morning."

"*What?*" Ivy's voice dropped.

Three sets of eyes were staring at Quinn.

"Are you serious?" Lissa said.

"Yeah."

"Ladies!" Mr. Fenner shouted across the gym. "Less gabbing, more stretching!"

Carmen stuck out a leg and bent over. "You're messing with us."

Quinn pulled a knee to her chin. "I'm not."

"Tommy Strout offered you a ride to school."

"Yeah. We met at the beach."

"Bull," Ivy said.

Quinn felt a churning in her stomach. She felt like she was back in Paige's basement on that One Stupid Night, trying to defend herself.

"I swear," she said. "I'm not making this up."

"We need details," Ivy said, just as Mr. Fenner blew his whistle.

"Ten laps, people! Now!"

They got up off the wrestling mat.

"Start at the beginning," Carmen said.

So Quinn started at the beginning. She told them how she'd decided to ride her skateboard to school. How she stopped off at Gulls Head Beach. How she was minding her own business, shooting free throws—

"Wait," Lissa said, slowing to a jog. "You play basketball?"

"Yeah."

"Like, on a team?"

"Yeah," Quinn said. She hadn't quit. Even after that One Stupid Night, when her own teammates started treating her like she had the Ebola virus, blood squirting out of her eyeballs, she kept playing.

"Carm plays, too!"

"Pick up the pace, people!" Mr. Fenner hollered.

"You play basketball?" Quinn asked Carmen, picking up the pace.

"Yeah," Carmen said. "We were pretty good last year, too. Ten and three."

"Not bad."

"Tryouts for the freshman team are in Octobah. You should—"

"Hellooo," Ivy said. "Can we stay focused here?"

"On what?" Lissa said.

"On Tommy offering Quinn a ride?"

"Right," Quinn said. She returned to the beach. The free-throw line. The pink fuzzy dice hanging from Tommy's rearview.

"It's true," Ivy said—grudgingly, Quinn thought. "He does have those fuzzy dice hanging from his rearview."

"Lucky!" Lissa squealed. "I can't believe you got a ride with Tommy Strout."

"Well, he offered," Quinn said. "I didn't actually take it."

"Get out!"

"You didn't take the ride?"

"Why wouldn't you take the ride?"

"I had my skateboard," Quinn reminded them.

"*So?*" Ivy said.

"I don't know. Nick seemed mad or something. I didn't think he wanted me to get in the car."

"Nick's always mad," Ivy said. "That's why I broke up with him."

. . . . .

"If you want to see what Nick was like before," Carmen said at lunch, "you need to check out his Instagram."

"And while you're at it," Lissa said, "check out Tommy's. You'll *wish* you took a ride in his cah."

"Seriously," Carmen said. "The beach volleyball picture? No shirt?"

"Oh my gawd," Lissa said. "No shirt."

"We would show you right now," Ivy said. "If our stupid school didn't block Instagram."

Quinn was late to sixth period. She didn't mean to be, but her head was so itchy she'd had no choice. As soon as lunch was over, she hurried to her locker and grabbed her backpack. She locked herself in the farthest bathroom stall and waited until the bell rang. Only when the girls' room was completely empty did she take Guinevere off, unstick the ten pieces of wig tape, dump a bunch of witch hazel onto a scratchy brown paper towel, rub it all over her head, wait for it to dry, stick on ten new pieces of wig tape, and put Guinevere back on.

It took forever.

"Sorry I'm late," Quinn said as she walked into study hall. The first person she saw was Nick Strout. He was hard to miss, parked at a larger-than-average desk to the left of the door. His face was so red and sweaty, and his hair was winging out at such ridiculous angles, that it looked like he'd just . . . well . . . run a marathon.

Quinn didn't mean to smile. It happened without her consent. It wasn't that the thought of a boy with no legs running 26.2 miles was so hilarious. It was that—and this was the truth—sometimes she smiled when she was nervous. Showing up tardy, smelling like witch hazel, wearing a wig that might or might not be on straight, led her to freeze in the doorway, grinning like an idiot.

"No problem," the study hall monitor said. "Take a seat."

Of course there was only one empty seat.

Of course it was next to Nick Strout.

Of course she was still smiling.

"What?" he snapped.

"Nothing."

"Is something funny?"

"What?" Quinn put on her Botox face. "No."

She looked around the room for someone friendly, but other than Nick and the study hall monitor, no one had even noticed her walk in. Everyone was wearing their earbuds, eyes on their screens.

"The curse of the twenty-first century," Quinn's dad liked to say. "The whole world is retreating into their separate pods." If Quinn's dad were in charge, they would all be wearing togas, greeting one another in the town square. *Salve, Brutus. Salve, Spartacus.*

Quinn pictured her own earbuds, wrapped up in a messy ball on her bedside table at home. *Crap.*

She unzipped her backpack and pulled out her book for English. *A Separate Peace.* She knew nothing about it, other than that her teacher said it qualified for their realistic-fiction unit.

I went back, Quinn read. Three words, not even the whole sentence, before Nick Strout snorted.

Quinn looked at him. "What?"

"That book blows."

"You've read *A Separate Peace*?"

Nick smirked. "You'll probably love it."

"Oh, yeah?"

"Yeah."

"What makes you say that?"

"I can just tell. You're the type."

"What *type*?"

"The type that would love that stupid book."

"Huh," Quinn said.

"That's right. Huh."

He was smirking again. Quinn's brain started yelling, *That's not a real smile! That's an Ethan Hess smile!*

"You don't know anything about me," she said.

"Who says I want to?"

For a second Quinn wanted to smack Nick Strout in the face with *A Separate Peace*. But then she remembered what Ivy had said about his chopped-off personality.

So she decided to let Nick Strout slide. Just this once.

CHAPTER

WHILE MO WAS GETTING JULIUS SETTLED at the kitchen counter with his after-school snack and his headphones, Quinn was curled up on the couch with her phone. She entered the username Lissa had scrawled on a napkin during lunch: gulls24qb. Unlike Quinn's Instagram account, which was set to private, this one wasn't. One tap, and there he was: Nick Strout, standing on the sand in his navy-blue swim trunks, holding a football.

Quinn wasn't sure why she was surprised to see him like this. It wasn't like after her hair fell out she'd suddenly started posting selfies of her bald head. In fact, all the pictures she had posted in the past year had been of inanimate objects. Her basketball. The mountains outside her house in Boulder. Anything but herself. So Quinn got why Nick Strout wasn't exactly dying to post a picture of himself in a wheelchair. Still, it was hard to reconcile the Nick from study hall with the image on her phone. Instagram Nick looked like a different person, not just in the beach picture but in every one that followed. Nick grinning with two other guys in football jerseys. Nick grinning in front of a bonfire. Nick grinning in a suit and tie, his arm around Ivy, who was wearing a short red dress. Nick's photos had dozens of comments, hundreds of likes.

Quinn sat there, staring at all those pictures, thinking, *What happened to you, Nick Strout?*

Well, she knew what had happened to him. It was a snowmobile accident. But she found herself wanting to know more. She found herself googling "Nick Strout Gulls Head Massachusetts."

And here was what she got:

NORTH SHORE—Gulls Head Middle School quarterback Nicholas Strout was announced Friday morning as the Bay State Junior Sportsman of the Year. Strout was presented with the award in a surprise announcement on WHGH, Channel 5, by former Boston College quarterback Ryan Barker.

"It's pretty crazy getting a plaque from a guy I idolized when I was little," Strout said. "I grew up watching Barker play. It's pretty cool."

Strout, an eighth grader at GHMS, went 237 of 348 this season for 3,603 yards and 44 touchdowns

while throwing just five interceptions. He led the Seagulls to the state D-3 semifinals, where they fell to Tewksbury Middle School, 37–34.

At the presentation Friday, the thirteen-year-old phenom credited his brothers, former Gulls Head High School QBs Gavin and Christopher "Kip" Strout and current JV QB Thomas Strout, and father, Marc Strout, with "teaching me everything I know about football." Strout said, "[My dad] was my first coach. He put a football in my hands when I was three and I've basically been throwing TDs ever since."

Then Quinn pulled up something else. A GoFundMe page entitled "Nick's Fight," dated May 19.

Dear Friends of Nicholas Strout,
We are writing with an update, not only on Nicky's progress, but also on our campaign to raise funds to support him in his rehabilitation and recovery. As you are aware, Nick suffered a crushing injury while snowmobiling on March 29 and has since undergone a bilateral above-knee amputation. Any amputation is life altering, but those with bilateral above-knee amputations face a host of complicated physical and emotional challenges. With your help, this GoFundMe campaign has raised nearly $8,000. Thank you so much for your support and generosity

so far. On behalf of the Strout family, we could not be more grateful.

The post went on to explain everything Nick would need going forward. Short prosthetic legs with training feet. Full-length prostheses with microprocessor-controlled knees, or computerized legs. Then came the costs: $2,000 for the basic components of each prosthesis, followed by prosthetists' fees of $10,000 to $15,000 per leg just for the basic models. The advanced computerized prostheses, controlled by muscle movements, would cost upward of $70,000 per leg, only a portion of which would be covered by the Strouts' insurance.

Seventy thousand dollars per leg? Quinn's wigs were nothing compared to this. She wondered what Nick's parents did for work. Most of the houses in Gulls Head were pretty small. Did they have savings? Would they need to take out a second mortgage? This was what Quinn's parents had done when Julius was accepted at the Cove. They'd remortgaged their house in Boulder and rented it out to pay for his school. Quinn wasn't supposed to know, but she'd overheard them talking one night, maybe a week before they moved. "What about Quinn's college?" her mom had said, and her dad had said, "We'll figure it out," and her mom had said, "I don't want her to have to pay back student loans like I did," and her dad had offered up one of his gems: *Improvidus, apto, quod victum.* Improvise, adapt, overcome.

Looking at Nick Strout's GoFundMe page, Quinn

65

wondered how he was "improvising, adapting, and overcoming" with the whole I-no-longer-have-legs situation. There had to be an online support group for amputees, right? If there was alopeciasucks.com, maybe there was amputationsucks.com. She tapped on Google again.

Wait—was it creepy what she was doing? Was she being a total freak show? Ivy and Lissa had cheer practice after school. Carmen had field hockey. What did Quinn have? Her extracurricular activity was googling a boy she barely knew and searching for imaginary websites. She needed to get a life.

But first, real quick, she'd hop back on Instagram and follow Nick Strout. She'd send follow requests to Ivy and Carmen and Lissa, too. This wasn't being a stalker. This was being a normal person.

Also normal: completing her geometry worksheet, reading three chapters of realistic fiction, and putting away her laundry.

. . . . .

When Quinn walked into the kitchen at five-thirty, her father was standing at the counter, slicing tomatoes, which confused her. "Dad?"

He looked up and smiled. *"Salve, filia."* Greetings, daughter.

"Salve," Quinn said. "Why are you home so early?"

"No one signed up for office hours. I caught the four-twenty train. Thought I'd help your mom with dinner."

"Oh."

He held up a slice of tomato. *"Cupis?"*

"Yeah, okay."

Julius was sitting at the kitchen table with his headphones on, humming to himself and holding a bunless hot dog.

Now Quinn was doubly confused. "It *is* Thursday, right?"

"Last I checked," her dad said, arranging tomato slices on a plate.

"Is he planning to put that hot dog in a thermos?"

Julius ate only out of a thermos on Thursdays. Thursday, thermos. It was an alliteration thing. Quinn had no clue how his brain came up with this stuff. Normally he chose foods that made sense in a thermos, like oatmeal.

"Shhh," Quinn's dad said, sprinkling salt on the tomatoes. "I'm trying something new."

That was when Quinn's mom marched into the kitchen, holding one of her clay busts. "Look at this," she said.

Quinn looked. The head appeared to have been scribbled on with blue marker.

"Every single one," her mom said. "Every. Single. One." She turned to Quinn's brother. "Julius?"

Of course, he couldn't hear her because he had his headphones on. Another mom might have raised her voice or yanked the headphones off her child's head to get his attention. Not Mo. She knew that if she startled Quinn's brother, or touched him the slightest bit, he would flip out.

67

"Buddy." Quinn's mom knocked gently on the table. She motioned for Julius to remove his headphones.

"I'm listening, Mo. *Indigo Dreams.*"

Indigo Dreams was this CD Quinn's parents had bought that was supposed to help her brother stay calm during transitions. It was not the weirdest thing they'd ever done. Back in Boulder, they had tried all sorts of alternative therapies. They'd taken Julius to this woman who claimed to remove toxic metals from autistic kids' bodies by playing different wavelengths of sound while they were sleeping. The first time Quinn's parents had tried it on Julius, he'd immediately started wetting the bed. So they'd moved on to Chinese medicine—acupuncture, acupressure, aligning the hemispheres of Julius's brain—which didn't seem to do anything. Next came the naturopath, who told Quinn's parents to eliminate casein and soy and gluten and all red foods from Julius's diet. If you asked Quinn, that was the reason he was so hung up on food. Right now, he was clutching his naked hot dog and looking around the kitchen. "Where's my thermos, Mo?"

Quinn snuck a glance at her dad, who said casually, "We'll talk about your thermos in a second, kiddo. Right now, look at Mo."

"It's already been a second, Phil," Julius said, looking at his hot dog. "A second has passed. Two seconds have passed."

"Julius," Quinn's mom said.

"Thermos Thursday, Mo."

"Yes, I know it's thermos Thursday, but I need to ask you a question." She lowered the clay bust to the table. It was one of her better works. Strong Roman nose. Full lips. Delicate ears. "Did you draw on this head with a marker?"

"Limited Edition Sharpie brand Color Burst Fine Point Permanent Marker, Mo. Jetset Jade."

"You drew on this head with Sharpie?" Quinn's mom said. "You drew on *all* my heads with Sharpie?"

"Not your head, Mo. You have hair." Julius was rocking in his chair, forward and backward, forward and backward, eyes on the hot dog.

"I see."

"No, you don't, Mo. You don't see your hair unless you look in a mirror. Your hair is above your eyes."

It was hard to argue with Quinn's brother's logic.

"Julius." Quinn's mom took an audible breath, let it out slow. "What is the rule about Mo's studio?"

"I don't go in Mo's studio."

"Did you go in Mo's studio?"

Quinn's brother didn't answer, just rocked.

"Julius," her mom said softly. "You drew on my art. That I worked very hard on. You drew on it with *permanent marker*."

"Limited Edition Sharpie brand Color Burst Fine Point Permanent Marker, Mo. Jetset Jade."

Oh, dear God.

"Where's my thermos, Mo?" His body was picking up speed.

69

"Julius," Quinn's mom said, "you're rocking. I would like you to stop rocking and look at me."

Quinn didn't know how her mother stayed so calm. Her art had been vandalized by her nine-year-old. It was crazy. Quinn would laugh if the situation were not, at least partially, her own fault. If she hadn't gone bald before his very eyes, she doubted that her brother would have done what he had. His heightened awareness of hair was the reason he'd defaced Mo's sculptures by giving them all Sharpie wigs. Quinn was sure of it.

"If you look at me, Julius, I will give you a sticker for eye contact. See? I have your chart right here."

Now Quinn had to laugh. She really did. Her mom was holding up a piece of poster board, pointing to a box with a pair of eyeballs in it.

"Thermos Thursday, Mo."

"How about this, Jules?" Quinn's dad said. He walked over to the table with one of their blue ceramic bowls. "Why don't you put your hot dog in here?"

"That's not a thermos, Phil. That's a bowl."

Quinn didn't know how her brother could see the bowl, between the rocking and the hot dog squeezing. His peripheral vision was impressive.

"It's *like* a thermos," Quinn's dad said. "See? You can put food in it. Your hot dog will fit nicely. *Fit perfectum.*"

"Phil," Mo said. She gave Quinn's dad a look.

If there was anything Quinn's father prided himself on

70

more than spouting random Latin phrases, it was reading Mo's cues.

"Gotcha," he said. He grabbed two tomato slices, handed one to Quinn, and gestured with his head for her to follow him out of the kitchen.

"Good luck, Mom," she said.

Mo gave Quinn a tired smile. "Thanks."

"Bye, Julius."

Just once, Quinn would like for her brother to look her in the eye and say something that made sense. Like *See ya*, or *Later alligator*. But all she got was "Thermos Thursday, Mo," directed at a hot dog.

Quinn followed her dad into the living room. When he sat on the couch and patted the space beside him, she sat.

"Quomodo erat dies tuus?"

Quinn looked at her dad. Phil's eyes were the blue of a swimming pool. His beard had a chunk of tomato in it. "Can we *please* speak English?"

He nodded. "Sure. How was your day?"

"Fine."

Quinn's phone pinged from the pocket of her shorts. When she reached for it, her dad said, "Can we please hold off on devices?"

"Sure," Quinn said.

Back in the kitchen, Julius was really revving up. "Thermos Thursday, Mo! Thermos Thursday!"

"The new plan's really working, huh?" Quinn said.

71

"These things take time," her dad said.

Quinn's phone pinged again.

"Let me just check this real quick," she said. "It might be about homework."

"Go ahead."

Quinn glanced at her phone.

Instagram now
Nick Strout (gulls24qb) accepted your follow request.

Instagram now
Nick Strout (gulls24qb) requested to follow you.

"Huh," Quinn said.

"Homework?"

"No." She slid her phone back in her pocket. "It's just this boy."

Her dad cocked an eyebrow. "There's a boy?"

"It's not like that," Quinn said. "He just wants to follow me."

"Follow you?"

"On Instagram."

"Ah."

As if Quinn's dad had a clue what following someone on Instagram meant. Phil had yet to enter the twenty-first century. He still had a flip phone. Half the time he forgot to charge it.

"What's this boy's name?"

"Nick."

"Nick," Quinn's dad repeated. "Tell me about Nick."

"He's just this kid in my study hall."

"And?"

"And . . . ," Quinn said. "There's tomato in your beard."

She said this because it was true. Also because she wasn't sure how much she wanted to tell her father about Nick Strout. *He doesn't have legs. He's kind of a jerk.*

"Right you are," her dad said, plucking the chunk of tomato from his beard and popping it into his mouth. Classic Phil.

"I don't want a sticker, Mo!" Julius hollered from the kitchen. "I want a thermos!"

"So much for the sticker system," Quinn said.

Her dad smiled. He reached out a long, thin hand and squeezed Quinn's elbow.

"What?" she said.

"Tell me more."

"More what?"

"More anything."

"I've only been in school for two days. There's not much to tell."

"Fair enough," her dad said. He shifted his gaze, not very subtly, from Quinn's eyes to her head. She knew he wanted to ask about Guinevere but he didn't know what to say.

"I'm fine, Dad. The wig's fine. I'm just not wearing it right now because it itches. I have to take breaks."

73

"Breaks."

"I have to let my skin breathe."

"Right." He nodded. "That makes sense."

Quinn's phone pinged again. Then again. "Um . . . Dad?"

"Go on." He waved his hand through the air. "Go be a teenager. Grab yourself a hot dog."

. . . . .

Instagram 7m ago
Nick Strout (gulls24qb) accepted your follow request.

Instagram 7m ago
Nick Strout (gulls24qb) requested to follow you.

Instagram 3m ago
Ivy D'Arcy (poisonivy710) accepted your follow request.

Instagram 3m ago
Ivy D'Arcy (poisonivy710) requested to follow you.

Quinn didn't respond to Nick's request right away. She accepted Ivy's follow and browsed through Ivy's photos. Ivy in a cheerleading skirt on top of a pyramid. Ivy in a cheerleading skirt, leaping through the air. Ivy smiling cheek to cheek with Lissa. Ivy smiling cheek to cheek with Carmen. Ivy smiling cheek to cheek with Lissa and Carmen.

And then—Quinn was surprised to see this—about fifty pictures of Ivy and Nick. Ivy and Nick in front of a fountain. Ivy and Nick making monkey faces. Ivy and Nick kissing.

It was weird to see. Because, well, wasn't there some kind of post-breakup protocol? Weren't you supposed to erase all evidence of your ex-boyfriend after you dumped him? Maybe, deep down, Ivy still had feelings for Nick. Maybe she wanted to make future boyfriends jealous. Whatever the reason, Quinn couldn't look away. She scrolled through every photo of Ivy and Nick. When she got to the end, she tapped out of Ivy's page. A second later she got:

Instagram now
gulls24qb sent you a direct message.

Quinn tapped the mail icon.

gulls24qb Y r u following me on IG?

Quinn tapped out her reply. Y not?
Right away, another ping.

gulls24qb IDK. B/c I'm a jerk?

Quinn let this answer sink in. When she didn't respond right away, she got this:

gulls24qb I haven't been very nice to u. I'm sorry.

Quinn thought about all the people in Boulder she would love to hear these words from. Like John Kugler, who once ripped the baseball cap off her head in the middle of all-school assembly and started a game of keep-away. And Mr. Davy, who saw her scalp shining in the light and everyone laughing and did nothing. And Sammy Albee, who posted the picture of Quinn on that One Stupid Night with the caption *gives new meaning to the word head*. Not one of them had ever apologized. But here was this guy Quinn had known for two days, already telling her he was sorry.

She looked at the words, and she imagined Nick Strout sitting in his wheelchair, frowning down at his phone with those dark, dark eyes, waiting for her reply.

And she wrote back, A real jerk wouldn't have apologized.

CHAPTER
7

THREE WEEKS INTO SCHOOL, QUINN'S MOM MADE her an appointment at the Shoreline North Medical Center.

"I won't be at lunch today," Quinn informed the girls during PE. "I have a checkup."

"Ortho?" Ivy asked.

It was a logical guess. Quinn's classmates seemed to get pulled out of Gulls Head High School all day long for orthodontist appointments. But Quinn, whose teeth were naturally straight, didn't want to lie. So she said, "Doctor."

This was the truth. Quinn was getting a checkup, and she was seeing a doctor, just not a pediatrician. She was seeing a dermatologist, like she'd seen Dr. Hersh back in Colorado, once when her hair first started falling out, and then again six months later.

Unlike Dr. Hersh, Dr. Kudirka of the Shoreline North

Medical Center was a woman. She had flowing brown hair, and she didn't wear a white coat. She wore jeans and a lavender T-shirt that read, *DERMATOLOGIST BY DAY, CAT LOVER BY NIGHT.*

"Nice to meet you, Quinn," Dr. Kudirka said, holding out a hand for Quinn to shake.

"Nice to meet you, too."

Quinn sat on the crinkly paper of the examination table, bareheaded. Mo sat on a chair in the corner, holding Guinevere in her lap like a small dog.

"So," Dr. Kudirka said, glancing at her clipboard. "You noticed your first bald patch fifteen months ago?"

Quinn nodded. Four hundred and twenty-nine days, but who was counting?

"And it took about eight weeks for the hair to fall out completely?"

"Yes."

"Have you noticed any regrowth since then?"

"No."

"Let's take a look, shall we?"

Dr. Kudirka flicked on a light that hung down from the ceiling like a spider's leg. She put on a pair of magnifying glasses just like the ones Dr. Hersh had worn. She peered at Quinn's scalp.

After a minute she said, "I don't see anything."

"You don't?"

"Not yet. No."

78

"Not yet," Quinn's mom repeated. "So there's still a chance the hair could grow back?"

"That's the good news about alopecia areata," Dr. Kudirka said, removing her glasses. "It's cyclical. No matter how widespread the hair loss, most hair follicles stay alive and are ready to resume normal hair production whenever they receive the appropriate signal."

The appropriate signal. Quinn wondered what this was but didn't ask. She had been sending signals to her hair follicles for over a year now. She had been speaking to them softly. *Grow, grow, grow.* She had been singing to them sweetly.

"The course of the disease," Dr. Kudirka continued, "is different for everyone, but we have every reason to hope that Quinn's hair will grow back. We just can't predict when that will happen or how long the regrowth will last."

"I see," Quinn's mom said.

"I know it's frustrating," Dr. Kudirka said, "but all we can really do at this point is wait."

We, Quinn thought. Like Dr. Kudirka was planning to sit around all day with Quinn and her mom, the three of them watching Quinn's hair follicles hibernate.

"I'm sorry, honey," Mo said, as soon as they were alone in the room.

"It's okay."

"I was hoping . . ." Mo's voice trailed off.

"I know," Quinn said. "It's fine."

She pulled a roll of wig tape out of her pocket. She ripped

off a piece with her teeth. Then another. After three weeks of dealing with Guinevere, Quinn was practically an expert.

"Do you need some scissors?" Quinn's mom asked.

"No." It felt good to use her teeth. It felt good to rip and tear.

"You don't have to go back to school," Mo said. "We could go out for ice cream." Like Quinn was still a little kid. Like ice cream could fix anything.

"Sure," Quinn said, slapping the wig tape onto her scalp with unnecessary force.

"Would you like that, honey?"

"I said sure."

. . . . .

On their way to the lobby, Mo's phone rang. She glanced at the screen before answering. "Sabine? Is everything okay?"

Sabine was a name Quinn had been hearing a lot lately. *Sabine says to focus on the positive. Sabine says to put play on the schedule. Sabine says to set small, measurable goals.*

"Can you hold on a sec, Sabine?" Mo said. To Quinn, she whispered, "It's Sabine, from the Cove."

Like there was any other Sabine.

"She has to talk to me about Julius . . . Here." Mo rifled through her purse and came up with a ten. "Why don't you find the café and get yourself something to eat? I'll join you as soon as I'm finished."

"Fine," Quinn said, taking the ten bucks like everything was cool—who cared about ice cream? Who cared about Julius ruling the world?

"Sabine?" Mo pressed the phone to her cheek. "What's going on?"

. . . . .

If the Shoreline North Medical Center had a café, it was in some top-secret location Quinn didn't know about. She wandered from floor to floor. Radiology. Pediatrics. Obstetrics. Health and Wellness. There was no food to be found. Not even a vending machine.

Quinn didn't really care. She wasn't hungry anyway. She was too busy thinking about her stupid bald head. She didn't want to think about it, but she was. And, as always, thinking about her stupid bald head made her think about that One Stupid Night and how it had ruined everything.

In the weeks that followed *gives new meaning to the word head*, Quinn kept thinking it would blow over. She would wake up each morning saying to herself, "Today will be different. Today, Paige and Tara will act normal. Today, the girls on my team will forget what happened and we'll go back to just playing basketball." Quinn kept waiting for someone to text her, to show up at her locker, to ask her to hang out after practice. But nothing happened. Life as Quinn McAvoy had known it was over. In the course of one night, she had become

Pluto: a has-been planet, too dwarflike and unimportant to hang with the other celestial bodies. She never mentioned this to her parents. Once, when they were having dinner, Mo looked at her across the table and said, "Are you okay, honey? You seem tired." Quinn had almost said it then. *I've been downgraded, Mom. I'm Pluto.* She had been about to open her mouth when Julius noticed a green pea in his mashed potatoes and flipped out. *White Wednesday, Mo! White Wednesday!*

Fast-forward six months. The morning Quinn's parents loaded up the U-Haul to make the trip from Boulder to Gulls Head, Quinn ran into Ethan Hess. Of course she did. It was Murphy's Law that on the same day she was moving away she would bump into the one person in the universe she least wanted to see, in the soda aisle of Lucky's Market.

She hadn't wanted to see him, yet there he was, reaching for a Dr Pepper. And she wasn't about to let this moment pass her by, so she headed straight for him. "That's what liars drink, huh?"

Ethan had looked up, surprised. "Quinn?"

"Oh, *now* you know my name?"

"What?"

"You heard me."

He looked so stupid all of a sudden, standing there with his floppy hair and his too long, too low shorts. Quinn had the crazy urge to pull down those shorts right there, in the middle of Lucky's Market, because that was what he deserved. But she restrained herself. She said, "I'm moving today."

"Yeah." Ethan nodded like a floppy-haired bobblehead. "I heard something like that."

"Is there anything you want to say to me before I go?"

"I . . ."

She opened her arms wide. "Here's your chance."

"Um," he said, looking around like he was afraid someone might see him talking to G. I. Jane and think he was a loser.

"It's just you and me, Ethan," Quinn said quietly. For a second, she let herself remember the first five minutes in Paige's bathroom, when the two of them been talking and laughing and she had actually hoped he would kiss her.

"Look, Quinn," he said. "I'm—"

"Dude!"

Suddenly, it wasn't just the two of them. John Kugler appeared out of nowhere. The same John Kugler who, just days before, had ripped the Colorado Rockies cap off Quinn's head in the middle of assembly and started a game of keep-away.

"What are you doing with the Head?" John smirked. "Coming back for more?"

"Yeah," Ethan muttered. "Right."

"Dude." John held out his hand for a high five.

"Wow, John," Quinn had said, her voice thick with sarcasm. "You're such a *nice guy*. You're both such *nice guys*. I hope all the boys in Massachusetts are just like you." She'd walked away to the sound of them cracking up, and even though she could tell that Ethan was only fake laughing, and she believed that he would have apologized if John hadn't shown up, it still hurt.

Even now, when Quinn McAvoy of Gulls Head, Massachusetts, thought about Ethan Hess or John Kugler or Sammy Albee or Paige or Tara or any of the girls on her basketball team, her stomach felt as holey as a hunk of Swiss cheese. Especially on days like today, when dermatologists in stupid T-shirts told her there was nothing to be done about her bald head, the dark thoughts swirled.

What if the wig tape doesn't stick?

What if Guinevere comes flying off?

What if everything that happened in Boulder repeats itself all over again?

These were the what-ifs playing on the screen in Quinn's brain when she passed a set of double doors leading into a room filled with light. The entire back wall was windows. Scattered all around were those brightly colored exercise balls, like the one Quinn's mom used to bounce Julius up and down on when he was a baby. There were a few people working out on weight machines. A blond woman lying on a cushioned table. A boy, about the same age as Julius, holding on to two wooden bars, taking halting steps forward on short metal legs.

It took Quinn a few seconds to register.

She knew that boy.

He was not the same age as Julius.

His legs were just really, really short.

Even though he was concentrating on the floor in front of him, he must have sensed her standing in the doorway because he looked up and froze.

Quinn knew, without Nick Strout saying a word, that he wanted to run, or evaporate, whichever would make him disappear faster.

This was the moment where, if Quinn were brave, she would rip Guinevere off her head and say, "Those are your legs? Well, this is my head."

But she couldn't do it.

She and Nick weren't friends yet. Not really. In the weeks since his Instagram apology, things had improved. She would admit that. They said hi to each other in study hall now. Once, when Quinn asked Nick for a Post-it, he gave her one. But that was all. Even Quinn's friendship with Ivy and Carmen and Lissa was too new, too unpredictable for her to bare all. Maybe there would be some magical moment in the future. Once she'd gotten to know everyone better. Once she knew she could trust them. But not here. Not now.

Now, Quinn would do something encouraging, but far less dramatic than ripping off her wig. She would give Nick Strout a thumbs-up. And then she would hightail it out of there.

CHAPTER

IN THE PARKING LOT OF THE COVE, while Mo was inside meeting with Sabine and Julius and whichever teacher Julius had spat on, Quinn took out her phone. She tapped on Instagram and sent a direct message to Nick.

Sorry for surprising u like that. I didn't know u would be in there.

Then she replied to the group text from Ivy and Carmen and Lissa. All ok. Dr's appt ran long. C u tmrw.

A minute later, Quinn's phone pinged.

Instagram now
gulls24qb sent you a direct message.

Quinn tapped on Instagram again. She hit the mail icon.

gulls24qb What were u doing there?

Dr's appt, Quinn wrote back.

gulls24qb What kind of dr?

Quinn thought for a second before she answered. Then she wrote, Dermatologist.

gulls24qb Y?

Quinn thought another second before answering. Skin stuff.

It wasn't even close to the whole truth. But Quinn didn't want to get into that, so she wrote something that was related to "skin stuff" but had nothing to do with bald heads or amputated limbs.

Did u know there's this guy in California who can stretch the skin from his neck all the way over his mouth? Quinn sent this message without really thinking about how weird it was.

Then a new message appeared.

gulls24qb Random.

So Quinn wrote another message, by way of explanation. My brother is obsessed w guinness world records. Trust me. They get way more random than that.

gulls24qb How random?

And Quinn wrote, IDK. Most toilet seats broken by someone's head in 1 min?

gulls24qb LOL.

The thought of Nick Strout laughing out loud made Quinn want to keep going. So she picked up one of Julius's books, which were sitting in a stack in the backseat, and she began flipping through, looking for the strangest records she could find.

Longest distance keeping a table lifted w teeth. Longest metal coil passed thru nose & out mouth. Most wins @ the world beard and mustache championship.

Quinn decided to stop there, in case Nick was starting to think she was a freak.

It took a few minutes, but then he replied.

gulls24qb There's a world beard and mustache championship?

And she wrote back, Apparently so.

gulls24qb I can't believe those r real records.

And she wrote back, Ikr?

Quinn realized—after her mom and Julius got back in the car and they all drove home—that she and Nick Strout had just broken their very own record. Longest conversation.

CHAPTER 9

QUINN WAS BOTH SURPRISED AND NOT SURPRISED when Nick was at the beach the next morning. "Hey," she said, skidding to a stop on the sand and hopping off her skateboard.

"Hey."

She knew not to smile. She knew not to stare. She knew that the last question in the world she should ask was *Why are you in your wheelchair if you have prosthetic legs?*

She had only one option: act normal.

Quinn dropped her backpack on the ground next to her skateboard. She dribbled to the foul line. *Bounce, bounce, catch. Bounce, bounce, catch.* She sank her ten free throws. When she dribbled back and Nick was still sitting at the end of the court, she said casually, "You want to pass?"

He shrugged. "Okay."

She bounced the ball between them, nice and easy.

He caught it and fired back a bullet.

"You have good hands," she said. Soft pass.

"I used to play football," he said. Hard pass.

"Oh yeah?" Medium pass.

"Quarterback." Hard pass.

"I can tell." Medium pass. "You want to play a lightning round?"

"What's that?" Hard pass.

Quinn held the ball to explain. "It's this thing we used to do at my basketball camp. Our coach would pass someone the ball and fire a question at the same time, like, 'What's your favorite color?' And that person had to pass the ball back right away, answering the question. Want to try?"

"Okay."

"What's your favorite color?" Quinn said as she passed the ball.

Nick caught it, passed it back. "Green."

"Favorite food." Pass.

"Tacos." Pass.

"Chicken or beef?" Pass.

"Either." Pass.

"Favorite animal." Pass.

"Cheetah." Pass.

"Ice cream?" Pass.

"Oreo." Pass.

"Candy." Pass.

"Black licorice." Pass.

"Seriously?" Quinn held the ball.

"Yeah."

"No one likes black licorice."

"I do."

Quinn smiled. She passed the ball back. "Favorite movie."

"Fletch." Pass.

"Song." Pass.

" 'Till I Collapse.' " Pass.

"Why don't you have an accent?" Pass.

"What?" Pass.

"A Boston accent." Pass.

"We moved here from Michigan." Pass.

"Oh yeah?" Pass.

"Where people say their *R*s." Pass.

Quinn smiled. "How old were you?" Pass.

"When I moved?" Pass.

"Yeah." Pass.

"Six." Pass.

"What happened to your legs?"

Nick made a loud, and kind of hilarious, *HO* sound as he caught the ball.

Quinn waited.

He passed the ball, but he didn't answer.

She passed it back, waiting.

"It was a party," he said finally. Pass.

Quinn nodded. Pass.

"We went snowmobiling." Pass.

Pass.

"Tommy was driving." Pass.

Tommy was driving? Pass.

"I was on the back." Pass.

Pass.

"We hit a patch of ice and flipped." Pass.

Pass.

"I got trapped underneath." Pass.

Quinn held the ball. Her brain was still back on *Tommy was driving.*

"I had a bunch of surgeries, and then I got this infection, and the tissue in my legs started dying, so—" Nick made a double chopping motion through the air. "That was it."

"I'm sorry," Quinn said.

"Yeah." He frowned at the ground. "Sorry doesn't change anything."

"I think it does. I think sorry is huge. I think saying it can change everything."

If there was one thing Quinn had learned from the suck-fest that was eighth grade, it was that. "I'm here because you said it . . . well, I'd be here anyway, but I wouldn't be talking to you."

Nick looked at her.

"The first time you messaged me," Quinn said, "on Instagram." She passed him the ball.

He passed it back.

"You apologized for being a jerk." Pass.

Pass.

"You know how many people in my life need to apologize for being jerks?" Pass.

"How many?" Pass.

"Rhetorical question." Pass.

"So?" Pass.

Now it was Quinn's turn to frown. She wasn't sure how much to say. *Look, Nick, you're not the only one who lost something.* Stupid. Well, true, but cheesy. And it wasn't like she was about to bare all in some act of solidarity, because that would be—

"Yo, Nicky."

Quinn was so relieved to see Tommy Strout and his duct-taped car pull up beside them, she actually cried out, "Tommy!"

"Hey, Quinn." That smile. "You want a ride?"

"Sure. Why not?"

Tommy hopped out of the car to help Nick in, just like last time. But this time Nick snapped, "I've got it."

Quinn busied herself with her backpack. She knew Nick was struggling to open the door, to heave himself into the backseat. But she pretended not to notice. She pretended to scrape something sticky—gum?—off one of her skateboard wheels while Tommy lifted Nick's chair into the trunk.

"Hey, Quinn," Nick said, when they were both belted in and Tommy was pulling out of the parking lot.

"Yeah?"

"You sure you want to ride with my brother?"

How was she supposed to answer that? Obviously she wanted a ride. If she didn't, why would she be in the car? "Yeah."

"You know he likes to drink and drive, right?"

"Nicky," Tommy said. Quinn could see his eyes in the rearview, right above the fuzzy dice.

"The faster the better."

Quinn looked at Nick. He was smirking.

"*Nicky,*" Tommy said again, sharper this time.

"What?"

"How many times are we going to do this?"

"I don't know, Tom. How long until my legs grow back?"

Nick's words hung in the air like a bad smell.

"Sorry, Quinn," Tommy said finally. "You shouldn't have to listen to this."

Quinn had no clue how to respond. *I don't mind?* She did mind. *I understand about family drama? About tense car rides? About brothers screwing up your life?* All of this was true, but she wasn't about to say it. So she said nothing.

Luckily, the ride from Gulls Head Beach to Gulls Head High School was less than a mile. In a matter of minutes, Tommy was pulling into the drop-off lane, and Quinn was getting out.

"Thanks for the ride," she said, flinging her backpack over

her shoulder, grabbing her skateboard, rolling her basketball onto her hip.

"Anytime," Tommy said. He was opening the trunk, lifting Nick's wheelchair out and onto the sidewalk.

When Quinn turned around, there were Ivy and Carmen and Lissa, standing on a patch of grass by the double doors. Three mouths gaping, three sets of eyes staring from Tommy to Quinn and back to Tommy.

Quinn waved. She tried to catch Nick's eye, but he wouldn't look at her. He was sliding out of the backseat, collapsing awkwardly into his chair.

"Sorry again," Tommy said, taking a step toward Quinn, giving her arm a squeeze.

"It's okay," Quinn said.

"I have to go park."

"Okay."

Quinn watched Tommy pull away from the curb. She started to turn toward Nick again, but the girls were upon her.

Ivy had a weird look on her face, like she'd tasted something sour.

Lissa was hugging Quinn around the neck, her mouth so close to Quinn's nose Quinn could smell her Juicy Fruit. "I am *so* happy for you."

"He squeezed your arm," Carmen said. "Tommy freaking Strout squeezed your arm."

. . . . .

"He likes you, you know," Carmen said in PE. "A boy doesn't touch a girl unless he likes her."

"He doesn't *like* me," Quinn said.

Lissa nodded. "Uh-huh. He does. We saw the whole thing."

Quinn glanced at Ivy, who was wearing her sour-lemon face again.

"You didn't see the whole thing," Quinn explained quickly. "You weren't in the car. Nick and Tommy were fighting. That's why Tommy squeezed my arm. He was apologizing for their fight."

"You don't need to squeeze someone's arm to apologize," Ivy said.

"You squeeze someone's arm," Carmen said, "if you want to squeeze them somewhere else."

Quinn laughed. "Right."

"Please, Tommy," Lissa whispered. "Squeeze me where I've nevah been squeezed before."

Quinn punched Lissa lightly in the shoulder. "Shut up. It's not like that."

. . . . .

"You know what would be awesome?" Ivy said at lunch.

"What would be awesome?" Carmen said.

"If Quinn got us invited to a varsity football party this weekend."

Quinn stopped peeling her banana. "How would I do that?"

"Two words," Lissa said. "Tommy and Strout."

"That's three words," Carmen said.

"No, it's not."

"You said, 'Tommy *and* Strout.' That's three words."

"You know what I meant."

"Can we stay focused here?" Ivy said.

When all eyes were on Ivy, she lowered her voice and said, "The football team has a bye this weekend."

"So?" Quinn said.

"So, whenever they don't have a game, they have a party. According to my sources, Jason Osternek's parents are going out of town this weekend."

"Who's Jason Osternek?" Quinn said.

"He's a senior," Carmen said. "He lives in the Strouts' neighborhood."

"He's having a party Saturday night," Ivy said, "and I thought, because of Quinn and Tommy's arm-squeezing connection—"

"We do not have an arm-squeezing connection."

Ivy sighed. "Did he or did he not squeeze your arm in front of school this morning?"

"He did, but—"

"You have an arm-squeezing connection. Deal with it."

"We should all be so lucky," Lissa said.

Quinn snorted. She took a bite of banana.

"So . . . what?" Carmen said. "You want Quinn to ask Tommy if we can come to the party?"

"Ding, ding, ding." Ivy rang an imaginary bell.

Quinn swallowed her banana. "How am I supposed to ask Tommy if we can come to a party? I don't even have his number."

"Easy," Ivy said. "Get it from Nick."

"Nick?"

"You guys have study hall togethah, right? You're *buddies* now?"

Maybe Quinn was imagining it, but Ivy sounded a little testy. "How do you know we have study hall together?"

Ivy shrugged, popping a few puffs of Pirate's Booty into her mouth. "Nick tells me everything. We may have broken up, but he still texts me, like, all the time."

"Well," Quinn said, "I wouldn't call us *buddies* exactly, but . . ."

Ivy rolled her eyes. "Just ask him for Tommy's numbah."

Quinn took a sip of milk. Was this some kind of test? If Ivy wanted Tommy's number so bad, why didn't she ask Nick herself?

"Not to sound lame," Quinn said, "but I don't think my parents will let me go to a party with no adult supervision."

Carmen laughed. "None of our parents will let us go to a party with no adult supervision."

98

"So . . . ," Quinn said.

"Two words," Lissa said. "Sleep ovah."

"That's one word," Carmen said.

"What are you, the word police?"

"I'm just messin'." Carmen blew Lissa a kiss. "You know I love you."

"*Anyway*," Ivy said. She grabbed Quinn's elbow. "You ask Nick for Tommy's numbah. You text Tommy, say you heard there was a party in his neighborhood, can you come and bring a few friends—"

"*Cute* friends," Carmen said.

"*Cute* friends," Ivy said. "Obviously. Then, once Tommy says we can come, you tell your parents you're sleeping ovah my house Saturday night. We eat snacks, watch movies, the whole nine, but as soon as my parents go to bed, we sneak out. Wicked easy."

"Lemon squeezy," Carmen said.

"Macaroni cheesy," Lissa said.

Quinn shook her head. "You guys are weird."

"So," Ivy said. "Will you do it?"

"Yeah," Quinn said. "Sure."

．　．　．　．　．

Quinn was early to study hall. She'd skipped her usual witch hazel routine in the bathroom so she could snag the seat next to Nick's. The bell hadn't even rung yet. Everyone was milling around, dropping backpacks onto the floor, laughing, looking at each other's phones.

After a minute or so, Nick rolled through the door.

"Hey," Quinn said.

He lifted his chin. "Hey."

He was trying to act cool, she could tell. Like the awkward car ride never happened.

"'Sup, dude," Nick said, which Quinn thought was overkill, but then she realized he wasn't talking to her. He was talking to someone behind her. A tall kid with bushy eyebrows and chapped lips.

"'Sup, Strout," the kid said. He and Nick bumped fists.

They nodded at each other a few times before the kid turned to Quinn. "I'm Griff."

"I'm Quinn."

"I heard. Colorado girl."

"Yeah."

Griff pumped his arm in the air. "Broncos!"

"Right."

"I'm a Pats fan myself. Like this guy here." Griff cocked his chin at Nick. "This guy coulda been the next Tom Brady. We used to tear it up, me and him. Back in the day. Right, Strout?"

Nick nodded.

Griff licked his chapped lips.

The bell rang. They fist-bumped again, and Griff took off

across the room to join some other kid in a football jersey. Nick looked like he'd shrunk six inches in his chair. The whole thing made Quinn's stomach hurt.

"Hey," she said to Nick, keeping her voice low even though everyone in the room had put in their earbuds. "Sometimes people just don't know what to say."

"What?"

She leaned in closer. "Sometimes people just don't know what to say, so they say weird things. They make an awkward situation even more awkward, but it's not like they mean to. They just can't think of anything else to do."

"Right," Nick muttered. "Like you would know."

Quinn thought about Paige and Tara and how, when her hair first started falling out, they pretended like they didn't notice, but then stupid comments would slip out of their mouths, like the time Paige told Quinn that her dog, Moose, got glue in his fur and had to have it shaved off, and then she'd looked at Quinn, all horrified, and said, *Ohmygod, I am so sorry.*

"I do know, actually," Quinn said.

"How?"

Quinn's brain scrambled around until it came up with an answer that wasn't about her hair. "My brother has autism," she said. This was how her mom had taught her to say it. *My brother has autism*, not *My brother's autistic*. Because, as Mo loved to say, *Julius is not defined by any one thing. He has many unique qualities.*

101

"The brother who's obsessed with Guinness World Records?"

"Yeah."

"There was an autistic kid in my class once," Nick said. "Second grade. He used to flap his hands."

"Julius does that sometimes. He kicks, too. It looks like he's dancing."

"Huh."

"He can't help it. That's just how his brain works. Most people don't understand. They have this picture in their head of what autism looks like. But my brother isn't . . . they call it a spectrum for a reason, you know? He doesn't fall into any one category. He's just . . . Julius. Sometimes, when we're out in public, people stare, or they make stupid comments. But it's not like they're trying to be mean. They just don't know how to act around him, you know?"

"Yeah," Nick said. "I think someone's trying to get your attention."

"What?"

He pointed to the door. Ivy's crazy ponytail appeared in the window, then disappeared, then appeared again. When Ivy caught Quinn's eye, she brought her hand to her ear, phone style.

"She wants you to call her," Nick said.

"No, she doesn't," Quinn said. "She wants me to ask you for Tommy's number."

"Why?"

Quinn shook her head. She felt dumb doing this, but she leaned in close to Nick and lowered her voice. "According to Ivy's *sources*"—she paused, scratching quote marks in the air with her fingers—"some kid named Jason is having a party this weekend? A football thing? His parents are going out of town?"

Nick gave Quinn a blank look.

"Anyway, if that's true, Ivy wants to come, and she thinks Tommy can get us invited."

"She's using you," Nick said.

"What?"

"Ivy's using you to go to a football party."

Quinn shook her head. "I don't think so."

"Trust me," Nick said. "She used to show up at my house after the accident. With Slurpees and Jolly Ranchers and whatever. She'd act like she was all concerned about me. And then, two seconds later, she'd be all, 'Where's your brother? Are his friends over?'"

"Maybe she felt awkward."

"Why would she feel awkward? She was my girlfriend."

"I don't know." How would Quinn have acted if Nick had been her boyfriend? If he had come home from the hospital with no legs, behaving like a different person? "Can I ask you something?" she said.

"Yeah."

"Was Ivy jealous?"

"What?"

"When you guys were going out. Was she jealous of you and other girls?"

"There *were* no other girls. If anything, I'm the one who should have been jealous. She was always drooling over Tommy and his friends."

Quinn nodded. "Right."

"I'm not giving you his number so you can become one of his little groupies."

"Fine," Quinn said. "Forget I said anything."

"If you want to go on Saturday night, just go. You don't need Tommy's permission."

"Really? We can just show up at some senior's house?"

Nick gave Quinn a funny look. "You're freshman girls. No one's going to turn you away."

CHAPTER
10

FuzzyWuzzy: Question. I'm going to a sleepover tonight where no one knows I am AAT. Can I sleep in my wig?

WigginOut: I have done it. Just be prepared u will have to brush all the tangles out in the AM otherwise u will be all matted and frizzed and it will be impossible to get them out later.

TheEyebrowsHaveIt: Agree. U will find the wig does flatten out and u will have to brush to keep looking good.

BaldFacedTruth: Even better if u sleep in a different wig than the one u wore during the day. If u have an older one that needs to b replaced soon u can wear that to bed.

T'sallGood: If ur going to use ur wig for sleeping make sure u wash and condition at least once a week

and remove any loose hairs and rinse the inside of
the cap really well b/c shampoo buildup can make ur
scalp crazy itchy.

HairlessWonder: I have not tried but have heard that
the fibers break down faster. But I'm sure doing it once
is no big deal. U can also use a cotton liner underneath
for sleeping. Super soft and stops the buildup of oils
from the scalp on the inside of the cap. I recommend
the 100% cotton wig cap from headcovers unlimited
but if u need something fast walmart has them too,
not cotton but ok in a pinch. Good luck!

TheNewNormal: Also recommend a satin pillowcase
so u don't wake up w/ major wig head. Otherwise no
problem. Throw on a little extra tape and i think you
will be fine and no one has to know. Don't worry and
Have Fun Fuzz!

T'sallGood: Good luck tonite!

BaldFacedTruth: Sleep tight ☺.

WigginOut: Have a ball!

That was the funny thing about alopeciasucks.com. Everyone was so enthusiastic and helpful, you almost forgot they
were a bunch of fellow baldies, hunched over their computers
and scratching their scalps. You were so busy picturing them
as flight attendants, smiling and passing out brushes.

Thanks for the tips, Quinn wrote back. I'll keep u posted.

"Tell me about Ivy," Quinn's dad said. They were in the car on their way to Ivy's house. Quinn had a sleeping bag in her lap, a new satin pillowcase in her backpack, and extra wig tape stuffed into a roll of socks.

"She's funny," Quinn said.

"Funny ha-ha or funny strange?"

"I don't know. Both."

"And your Hispanic friend? I forget her name . . ."

"Carmen, Dad. And she's not Hispanic. She's Dominican."

"Ah. *Dominican.*" Quinn's dad said *Dominican* with a Spanish accent, which was horrifying.

"Please don't talk like that when you meet her," Quinn said. "And don't say *salve* to Mrs. D'Arcy, either."

"No Latin?" Quinn's dad looked disappointed.

"No Latin."

. . . . .

Ivy's mom greeted Quinn and her dad at the door. She wasn't much taller than Ivy, and she wore her hair in two bushy ponytails, which made her look like either a really old toddler or a really young forty-year-old.

"You must be Quinn!" She came in for an unexpected hug. "I've heard so much about you!"

"Yes," Quinn said, her voice muffled by the sleeping bag jammed into her face. "You, too."

"And you must be Quinn's dad," Mrs. D'Arcy said, releasing Quinn and reaching out a hand that looked just like Ivy's, tan with lots of rings. "Hawahya? I'm Caroline D'Arcy."

"Phil McAvoy," Quinn's dad said.

Quinn could tell it was killing him not to say *vos noscere*.

"The girls are in the kitchen, Quinn," Ivy's mom said. "They'll be thrilled to see you."

Quinn said goodbye to her dad. She carried her backpack and sleeping bag through the hall.

Ivy, Carmen, and Lissa were gathered at a wooden table in the D'Arcys' kitchen. They were all wearing pointy yellow hats and digging their fingers into a tube of cookie dough.

"Quinn!" Lissa said when she saw Quinn standing in the doorway. "You made it!"

"I made it."

"Hey, Quinn," Carmen said, waggling her cookie-doughed fingers in the air.

"Hey."

"Good," Ivy said. "You brought a sleeping bag." She pointed to a door. "You can throw your stuff in the basement."

Quinn headed downstairs. The D'Arcys' basement wasn't very big—nothing like Paige's—but it had soft green carpet and movie posters everywhere, which was pretty cool. Quinn dumped her sleeping bag and backpack in the pile of other sleeping bags and backpacks and headed back up.

"You need a hat," Ivy said, springing from her chair and grabbing a pointy yellow hat off the counter.

"I didn't know it was your birthday," Quinn said.

"It's not."

"It's tradition," Carmen explained. "We've been doing it forevah."

And Ivy said, "First one to take off her hat has to do a dare. Last time it was Liss and we made her run around the block naked."

"Don't remind me," Lissa said. "Some old dude was out walking his dog. His eyes about popped out of his head."

"Gross," Quinn said.

"Take it from me," Lissa said. "Keep your hat on."

Quinn hooked the elastic strap under her chin and perched the hat on her head. Gently. Ten pieces of wig tape, but still. She wasn't taking any chances.

"Cookie dough?" Ivy held up a blob on her finger.

"Sure." Quinn helped herself to the blob. She pulled out a chair.

The four of them ate cookie dough until there was nothing left. They plowed through a bag of Cool Ranch Doritos. They drained a liter of Mountain Dew.

Then Lissa unzipped her duffel bag. She held up a box with her skinny white arms. "It's Ouija time."

"Oh my gawd, yes," Ivy said.

"Let the spirits be moved," Carmen said.

Quinn hadn't seen a Ouija board since fifth grade. She

thought maybe this was a joke, but Ivy was actually walking around unplugging the toaster and the coffeemaker to avoid any "electrical disturbances with the spirit realm." Carmen was pulling incense and votive candles out of a paper bag, lighting them with the same kind of lighter Quinn's dad had used for their fireplace in Boulder.

Now, in the 85 percent darkness of Ivy's kitchen, Quinn watched Lissa place the Ouija board on the table. It looked just the way Quinn remembered. The letters of the alphabet in two arced rows over a straight line of numbers. The words *YES* and *NO* in the top corners. *GOOD BYE* at the bottom.

"Who should we summon?" Ivy said.

"Grandma Rosa?" Lissa said.

Ivy shook her head. "I'm sick of Grandma Rosa. No offense, Carm."

"None taken."

"She made the best tostones."

"I know she did."

Quinn had to ask. "What are tostones?"

"They're fried plantains," Carmen explained. "Served with this pickled hot peppah sauce. I could eat some right now."

"Me, too," Ivy said.

"What about that girl?" Lissa said, laying her fingers on the Ouija board.

"What girl?"

"When you guys were in third grade. Before I moved here. That skiing accident. What was her name? Andrea? Angela?"

110

"Allison Mercury," Ivy said.

"Oh yeah," Carmen said. "I forgot about Allison Mercury."

"How could you forget about Allison Mercury? She's the reason our mothahs are obsessed with helmets."

Quinn, who had been listening in silence, watching the candle flames flicker, had no choice but to ask. "Who's Allison Mercury?"

Carmen locked eyes with Quinn across the table. "She was in fourth grade when we were in third. She went skiing at Berkshire East and skied into a tree and hit her head. She was in a coma for three days and then she died."

"That's awful," Quinn said.

"I know," Carmen said. "Her family moved away right aftah."

"We should summon her spirit and see how she's doing," Lissa said.

Everyone agreed, and it was decided that Ivy and Carmen should do the summoning because, "back in the day," Ivy's cousin Bobby had been friends with Allison's brother Kai, and because Carmen had gone to Sunday school with Allison at St. Margaret's.

They rearranged the seating at the table so that Ivy and Carmen could sit across from each other with their fingers on the board.

"Allison Mercury," Ivy said softly. "Are you out there?"

"Allison Mercury," Carmen said. Her voice was deep like a preacher's. "We summon your spirit. Can you hear us?"

Quinn knew it was silly. She didn't believe in spirits. She knew that it was Ivy and Carmen who were making the little plastic thingy move toward *YES*. But there was something about the candles flickering in the dark and the silence of Ivy's kitchen that made the little hairs on Quinn's arms stand at attention.

"We see that you are here, Allison," Carmen intoned. "We can feel your presence."

"Hello, Allison," Ivy said.

"Hello, Allison," Carmen said.

And Lissa whispered, "Ask her how her head is."

Quinn could feel a snort rising in her throat. Then her phone pinged, saving her. She had meant to put it on silent earlier, but while everyone else was silencing their phones she had been adjusting the hat on her head because she felt like the elastic was pulling on some of Guinevere's hairs. Maybe she was paranoid, but she didn't want to chance it.

Her phone pinged again.

"Whose cell is that?" Carmen looked around the table. "It's killing the mood."

"Sorry," Quinn murmured. She reached into the pocket of her shirt to pull her phone out.

Instagram now
gulls24qb sent you a direct message.

She tried to press the button to power down, but she wasn't fast enough.

"Do you have a direct message from *Nick Strout*?" Ivy said, grabbing the phone out of Quinn's hand.

"Hey." Quinn reached out to grab it back, but Ivy stood up. Her fingers flew across the screen.

" 'Largest gathering of people dressed as Mahatma Gandhi. Most live rattlesnakes in your mouth.' What is this? It sounds kinky."

"Give it back," Quinn said, reaching for the phone again, but Ivy danced away.

"Are you getting kinky with my ex-boyfriend?"

The Ouija board was forgotten. Allison Mercury was forgotten. Everyone was staring at Quinn.

"Let me see that," Carmen said, and Ivy slid the phone across the table, too fast for Quinn to intercept.

She knew it wasn't the same as John Kugler ripping the Colorado Rockies cap off her head and all the eighth-grade boys playing keep-away. She knew it, and yet this felt the same. This felt, just for a moment, like her scalp was shining in the light and everyone was laughing.

"Give it back!" Quinn said, a lot louder than she'd intended.

"Sheesh," Carmen said, handing over the phone. "Take it easy."

Quinn lowered her voice. "There's nothing *kinky* about

those messages. It's just this stupid thing we were doing. Sending Guinness World Records back and forth."

"Why?" Carmen said.

"I don't know. We were bored in study hall one day." Quinn glanced at Ivy. She had that look on her face again, like she'd sucked on a lemon.

"Did I do something wrong?"

Ivy shrugged. "What would you have done wrong?"

"Do you not want me hanging out with Nick in study hall?"

"You can hang out with anyone you want," Ivy said. "It's a free country."

Quinn was getting a pit in her stomach. She didn't like the edge in Ivy's voice. Apparently no one did, because Carmen blurted out, "Study hall's the worst."

And Lissa said, "The worst."

"It's not like anyone actually *studies*," Carmen said. "So what's the point?"

"There *is* no point," Lissa said.

Quinn slipped her phone back in her pocket.

"Hey, Ive," Carmen said. "What time is it?"

Ivy held up a candle so she could read the clock on the wall. "Eight thirty-seven."

"How long until your parents go to bed?" Lissa said.

"I don't know. Two hours?"

"*Two hours?*" Carmen groaned. "How are we going to kill *two hours?*"

114

"We could watch a movie," Ivy said.

"Oooh, yes," Lissa said.

"Only if it's something good," Carmen said. "Not like that *You're So Cupid* crap we watched last time. Have you seen that one, Quinn?"

Quinn shook her head.

"You dodged a bullet."

"We should watch something scary so we don't fall asleep," Lissa said. "*Cabin in the Woods?*"

"That wasn't scary," Carmen said.

"*Scream?*"

"Nah."

"You guys want scary?" Quinn said. Now that the tension had lifted, she felt better. "Have you ever heard of *The Blair Witch Project?*"

. . . . .

Two hours later, they were sneaking through the woods behind Ivy's house, following the light from Ivy's phone.

"I can't believe you made us watch that movie, Quinn," Lissa said, clutching Quinn's hand.

"'I'm scared to close my eyes,'" Quinn said, in her best Heather Donahue voice. And Carmen said, "'I'm scared to open them.'"

"It is literally pitch-black out here," Lissa said. "Whose idea was it to walk through the woods anyway?"

115

"Ivy's," Carmen said.

"We'll never make it out alive," Lissa said.

"Trust me," Ivy said. "It's a shortcut."

They crossed through some backyards and dashed down a few side streets before they turned a corner and Ivy said, "See? We're already here."

Jason Osternek's house was lit up like a cruise ship. Cars were parked all along the street. People were standing out on the lawn. A few were smoking cigarettes.

"What about our hats?" Lissa said.

"What *about* our hats?" Ivy said.

"Are we still wearing them?"

"Of course we're still wearing them. It's tradition."

"Tradition's tradition," Carmen said.

"Right." Lissa nodded. She checked her hat.

Ivy and Carmen checked their hats. Quinn pretended to check her hat, but really she was checking Guinevere.

"Who wants gloss?" Carmen said. She unzipped her purse under the streetlight. "I've got options."

They took a few minutes to gloss up. They checked each other's teeth. Lissa passed out Tic Tacs.

"All right, girls," Ivy said finally. "Enough stalling."

"Let's do this thing," Carmen said.

They crossed the road and walked up the sidewalk. Standing on the porch, watching Ivy ring the doorbell, Quinn suddenly felt like a trick-or-treater. When the door flew open, she had the crazy urge to laugh.

"Nice hats!" yelled the boy who was standing in the foyer. He had a scruffy chin and a gold chain around his neck. He looked old enough to be in college.

"Thanks!" Ivy yelled back.

The music was so loud. Rap, not Quinn's favorite. She could feel the bass thumping in her stomach.

"Beer's in the basement!" Scruffy Chin yelled. He handed Ivy four red plastic cups.

"Thanks!" Ivy yelled again.

She led the way down the hall, but instead of heading down to the basement, she pulled everyone into a bathroom and shut the door behind them.

"*Beer?*" Lissa said. The music was muffled now, so they didn't have to yell to be heard.

"Of course beer," Ivy said. "It's a high school party."

"We're not going to *drink* it, are we?"

"Of course not. We're fourteen."

Ivy unzipped her shoulder bag. "I've got OJ, apple, cran-raspberry, and passion fruit."

They poured juice into their cups.

"If you need a refill," Ivy said, "just tell me and we'll meet back here. No one will bug you if your cup is full."

"Even if it's not beer?" Lissa said.

"Just tell them you're drinking a cocktail," Ivy said. "Now listen. I know from my cousin Bobby, crazy shiz happens at high school parties. We are not here to do crazy shiz. Repeat after me: *we are not here to do crazy shiz.*"

117

"We are not here to do crazy shiz."

"Right," Ivy said. "We are here to *observe* the crazy shiz, so when we're seniors we know what to do."

"Can we flirt with cute boys?" Carmen said.

"Flirting is encouraged," Ivy said.

"Can we kiss them?" Lissa said.

"If the opportunity presents," Ivy said, "yes."

Everyone looked at Quinn.

"Why are you looking at me?"

"Two words." Carmen waggled her eyebrows. "Tommy and Strout."

Before Quinn could protest, Ivy opened the bathroom door. Eminem blared. A river of bodies engulfed them.

Ivy and Carmen and Lissa and Quinn followed the current down to the basement. It wasn't deafening down there, but the music was still loud enough for people to be dancing—if you could call it dancing. Mostly what they were doing was grinding on each other while holding their red plastic cups in the air. A few girls were lounging on a couch. There was a keg of beer in one corner with a bunch of boys standing around it. Quinn didn't see Tommy or Nick anywhere.

"Oh my gawd!" said one of the couch loungers, waving her red plastic cup. "There are children here."

And her friend, a girl with streaky blond hair, said, "When's pin the tail on the donkey? When are the sack races?"

"Where's the balloon man?"

"Where are the cupcakes?"

They were cracking themselves up.

"I'm rethinking the hats," Ivy murmured.

"Thank you," Lissa murmured back. "Can we take them off now?"

"In a sec. Keep walking."

They followed Ivy to an empty patch of wall.

"Just to be clear," Carmen said, "I won't have to do a dare if I take this off?"

"No one will have to do a dare," Ivy said. "We'll take them off at the same time. One . . . two . . . three."

Ivy, Carmen, and Lissa removed their hats. Quinn took a sip of juice.

Everyone looked at her.

"You're keeping it on?" Ivy said.

"Yeah," Quinn said.

"Why?"

Quinn shrugged. "I like it."

The truth was, she felt like an idiot and the elastic was digging into her chin, but there was no way she was taking this pointy yellow hat off in the middle of all these people. She could just picture it, Guinevere getting caught on a staple, veering off to the side like a skidding car.

"I respect that," Carmen said.

They stood against the wall, sipping their juice. Over by the keg, some guy was standing on his hands, drinking beer out of the hose.

Ivy nudged Quinn's arm. "Did you ever see a party like this?"

119

"Only on TV."

The last party Quinn had gone to was that One Stupid Night, when she'd been wearing an equally strange hat that Ethan Hess had ripped off her head in front of everyone. But Quinn didn't want to think about that right now, and luckily she didn't have to because her phone was vibrating in her pocket.

How are you, honey? Are you having a good time at your sleepover? xoxo, Mom

Quinn felt a twinge of guilt as she texted back. Having a gr8 time. Thx. Will c u tmrw.

"Cute hat."

Quinn looked up from her phone, and *bam*, there was Tommy Strout, holding his red plastic cup.

"Hi," she said.

"Hi." Tommy's hair was dark and damp. His eyelashes were ridiculous. His smile was slow and beautiful. "Nick told me you might be coming tonight. I'm glad you made it."

"You are?" she said.

"I am."

Quinn could smell the beer on his breath, but she didn't mind. Tommy Strout was a perfect specimen of high school boy. If Quinn were a perfect specimen of high school girl, she might reach out and grab his face right now, pull it toward her, and kiss him on the mouth. But she wasn't. Quinn was nowhere near perfect. Nothing she was wearing—not the hat, not the wig, not the lip gloss, not the tight white shirt Ivy had lent her for tonight—felt like her. Quinn wondered what Tommy would do if she took off her "cute hat" right now and Guinevere came with it. She bet it would knock the smile right off his face.

Quinn glanced around the basement for Ivy and Carmen and Lissa. She didn't see any of them.

"Looking for Nick?" Tommy said.

"Yeah," Quinn said. Even though she hadn't been looking for him, the thought of seeing Nick made Quinn breathe easier. If anyone would be less comfortable than she was right now, it would be him.

"He's not here," Tommy said.

"He's not?"

Tommy shook his head. "But we live two streets over. Fifty-Four Chestnut. The front door's unlocked if you want to go say hi."

"Really?"

"Sure."

"What about your parents?"

"They go to bed early. Nick's in the den. First room on the left when you walk in."

"Okay. Thanks." Quinn started walking away. *Fifty-Four Chestnut*, she repeated to herself. *First room on the left.*

"Hey, Quinn."

She turned around. "Yeah?"

"Be good to my brother. He's been through a lot."

"I know," she said. What did Tommy think she was going

121

to do? Ring the doorbell and then run away laughing when Nick answered the door?

Quinn wove her way across the basement and up the stairs. She still didn't see Ivy or Carmen or Lissa. On her way outside, she texted them. Where r u guys??? Heading to Nick's house. Txt me back. Ivy might be mad, but Quinn wasn't going to worry about that now.

She sent Nick a direct message on Instagram. U up? I'm in ur hood.

Then she tapped on her navigation app and plugged in 54 Chestnut Street.

CHAPTER
11

TOMMY WAS RIGHT; THE FRONT DOOR was unlocked. Quinn walked in. She poked her head through the first doorway on the left. Nick was sitting on a pullout couch, a crocheted blanket on his lap, reading a book.

"Hey," Quinn said. She took two steps forward.

Nick looked up and frowned. "You should go back to the party."

"Why?"

"I know my brother sent you here to check on me. Like I'm some grandma in a nursing home."

"Tommy didn't send me."

"He didn't?"

Quinn shook her head. "I sent myself. He just told me where you live."

"Well, I'm fine," Nick said. "As you can see."

"I'm not."

"What?"

"I'm not fine," Quinn said. "The music was too loud, and I don't drink beer, and I lost my friends, and I felt really . . . I don't know . . . young."

"Could it be the hat?"

Quinn looked at Nick. He was smiling. An actual smile, not a smirk.

"Maybe," she said. She took his smile as an invitation to walk farther into the room, which was full of dark wood and plaid slipcovers and framed photos on the walls. "Are these all your brothers?" she asked, pausing at a shot of four boys in football jerseys, mugging for the camera.

"Gavin, Kip, Tommy, and me," Nick said. "In that order. I'm the one with no teeth."

"Cute."

There were school photos, of course, each boy through the ages. Glasses and braces and pimples and goofy grins. There were awkward family poses in front of the Christmas tree, everyone dressed in red, one where Nick was crying and his brothers were laughing.

"Awww," Quinn said. "What happened here?"

"Who knows? They did so much crap to me over the years I can't remember. One time, when I was four, my parents were out, and my brothers zipped me in a suitcase and pushed me down the stairs. My knee hit my mouth and knocked out my two front teeth."

"Really?"

"Yup."

"Even Tommy?"

Nick nodded. "Tommy followed Kip's orders. Kip followed Gavin's. And Gavin followed the General's."

"The General?"

"My dad."

"He's in the army?"

"Nah. General contractor. Construction sites."

"Oh," Quinn said. She leaned in to examine one of the family photos. Nick's dad had thick shoulders and one of those short, bristly haircuts. His eyes were squinty and his mouth was a straight line. *Game face*, Quinn thought.

She kept walking, pretending not to notice Nick's prosthetic legs propped in a corner. Instead, she stopped at a desk that was covered in papers. She started flipping through them.

"What are you doing?"

"Being nosy."

Quinn flipped and stared. Feet, calves, knees. Charcoal, ink, pastel. Broad strokes and delicate lines. Tendon, muscle, bone.

"Don't," Nick said sharply.

Quinn lifted her head to look at him. "Did you draw these?"

He nodded, almost imperceptibly.

"Nick. These are . . . amazing. I had no idea you were an artist."

"I'm not."

"Are you kidding?"

He shook his head. "I just like to draw."

"That's like Steph Curry saying 'I just like to play basketball.'" Quinn held up one of the foot sketches. "Do you know how hard this is? To get the shapes right? To add dimension? Whenever I try, I end up with a blob."

"You draw?"

Quinn smiled. "I doubt you could call it drawing. I take that studio art elective, fourth period? I'm really bad. My mom's the artist in the family. She's a sculptor. Heads and busts, mostly—"

"For a job?" Nick said.

"Yeah."

"Your mom actually makes money from doing art?"

"Well, she did in Colorado. I doubt she will here."

"What does she work with? Plaster? Terra-cotta?"

Quinn tried not to look surprised. "Clay, mostly."

"Does she have her own studio?"

"Yeah. It's just a room in our house, but . . ." Quinn looked at Nick. She was still trying to process the words coming out of his mouth. "You could come see it sometime, if you want."

"Really?"

"Sure."

Nick nodded. "Cool."

Silence for a second. Then he said, "I thought you would think I was weird."

"I do think you're weird."

"Shut up. I'm being serious."

"Okay."

"Drawing pictures of . . . you know . . . legs."

Quinn kept her eyes on Nick. Part of her wanted to look away so he wouldn't feel self-conscious, but the other part wanted to stay right here.

"I don't think you're weird," she said. "Not for that."

"You don't?"

"No."

The room was so quiet. Bizarrely quiet. And then it wasn't. There was a tapping sound, coming from outside.

"What's that?" Quinn said.

"I don't know."

The front door opened and Ivy came flying into the den. "The cops busted the party! We have to go!"

"The cops?" Quinn said.

"Yes!" Ivy hesitated for a second, then turned to Nick and gave him a strangely formal nod. "Hello, Nick."

"Hello, Ivy."

"Come on!" Ivy grabbed Quinn by the hand. "The girls are outside!"

"Bye, Nick," Quinn said, letting Ivy pull her out the door.

"Bye, Quinn."

. . . . .

Back in Ivy's basement, zipped safely into their sleeping bags, they couldn't stop laughing. "Ivy was like, 'The cops are here! We have to go!' And I was like, 'Can I please finish kissing this boy?'"

Carmen, apparently, had kissed a boy.

"Tell me again how it happened?" Quinn said. "How do you go from 'Hi, I'm Carmen' to letting him stick his tongue in your mouth?"

"To be fair," Carmen said, "he didn't use a lot of tongue."

"How much?" Lissa said.

"I don't know. A medium amount."

"What if the cops hadn't come?" Ivy said. "What if he'd tried something else?"

"Like what?"

"Like . . . up the shirt?"

"I'd have said, 'Easy, tigah, we just met.'" Carmen was sitting up in her sleeping bag, brushing her thick black hair. When she saw Quinn watching, she held out her brush. "You want?"

"No, thanks," Quinn said, feeling her cheeks go warm. She had, thank God, finally taken off her party hat. In the privacy of Ivy's upstairs bathroom, she had witch-hazeled her scalp, applied fifteen pieces of fresh wig tape, and pressed Guinevere on so hard her fingertips had turned white. Now she looked just like the rest of her friends, in flannel PJ bottoms and a T-shirt, holding her satin pillowcased pillow in her lap.

"Speaking of kissing . . ." Ivy turned to Quinn.

"What?"

"Is there anything you want to tell us?"

"About kissing?"

"We're confused," Ivy said. "First you're messaging Nick. Then you're flirting with Tommy in the basement. Then you're leaving Tommy in the dust to hang out with Nick."

Quinn inhaled. Quinn exhaled. She wasn't sure what Ivy was trying to say exactly, but it didn't sound good.

"I wasn't *flirting* with Tommy," Quinn said. "He's too old for me."

"He's not too old for *me*," Lissa said.

Carmen laughed. Ivy and Quinn didn't.

"We were just having a conversation," Quinn said. "And I didn't 'leave him in the dust.' He's the one who suggested I go see Nick after you guys ditched me."

"We didn't ditch you," Ivy said. "We went to refill our juice."

"How was I supposed to know that? You could have texted."

Carmen wrapped an arm around Quinn. "We were trying to be good friends. We wanted to leave you and Tommy alone so you could make out."

Quinn shook her head. Why did people always assume things about her that weren't true? She took another breath, let it out slow. "If I were going to kiss someone, it wouldn't be in a basement full of people. And anyway, it's not like that. Tommy and I are friends. *Nick* and I are friends." Quinn turned to Ivy. "I would never do that to you."

"Do what?"

"Steal your ex-boyfriend."

"Steal my ex-boyfriend?" Ivy's eyebrows shot up.

"Or your ex-boyfriend's brother, or whatever. I don't know. I'm confused, too."

Ivy huffed out a breath. "Oh my gawd, Quinn."

"What?"

"Am I being a total bee-atch?"

Quinn didn't know how to answer that, so she said nothing.

"You have no idea how awful it was," Ivy said softly. "After Nick's accident, it was like he had that thing that happens to soldiers when they come home from war . . . that disorder . . ."

"PTSD?" Carmen said.

"Right. He, like, couldn't stop crying, and he wanted me to be with him every second, but he nevah wanted to leave the house. It would be this beautiful sunny day, and all he wanted to do was stay inside, wrapped in a blanket. Every time I tried to leave, to go to the beach or whatevah, he would beg me to stay. Or he'd get really mad. It was like . . . I was everything to him. I was his lifeline. Do you have any idea what that felt like?"

Quinn shook her head.

"But now he doesn't need me anymore, and—"

"I'm sure he still needs you," Quinn said.

Ivy waved her off. "I know it sounds stupid. I'm the one who broke up with him. And I'm *glad* I broke up with him. It wasn't my job to sit in a dark room with him all summah long, you know?"

"It's not like you were married," Carmen said.

"It's not like you took vows," Lissa said.

"Right." Ivy nodded. Her face was serious. "But Nick was my first boyfriend. I cared about him. I *still* care about him. And his family. Not that Tommy ever gave me the time of day, the way he does with you." She looked at Quinn and shrugged. "But anyway . . . I guess I'm just kind of jealous that you got to roll into town and take my place."

Quinn thought about this. Ivy didn't sound like a bee-atch, exactly. She sounded honest.

"I'm not trying to take your place," Quinn said.

"I know you're not *trying* to."

"Do you want me to . . ." Quinn hesitated. "What do you want me to do?"

Ivy sighed and shook her head. "Nothing. You're not doing anything wrong. This is just me being stupid."

"I don't think you're being stupid," Quinn said. "It actually makes sense, the way you said it."

"Yeah?"

"Yeah."

Lissa nodded. "It makes total sense."

"You can't help how you feel," Carmen said.

"I don't know." Ivy sighed and collapsed back onto her pillow. "Maybe I just need someone new to kiss."

Lissa squealed. "Yes! New lips!"

"Someone older, without any emotional baggage."

"Like Rob," Carmen said.

"Who's Rob?" Ivy said.

"The boy I kissed tonight. He's definitely older."

Ivy sat up. "You want me to kiss *Rob*?"

"No. Rob's mine. You need to find your own Rob."

"I want a Rob," Lissa said. "Can we time-share?"

This made Ivy laugh.

"Rob has friends," Carmen said. "Did you see how cute some of them were?"

They burrowed deep into their sleeping bags and talked about the party. How cute the junior and senior boys were, and how mean the junior and senior girls were, and how lame the music selection was. When Lissa started sharing her list of the best dance songs and telling them that, if she ever had a party, these were the songs she would play, Quinn let her mind wander. For some weird reason, she kept coming back to Nick's hair. How it winged out from his ears like a little kid's, and how, the whole time they were talking tonight, she'd wanted to reach out and touch it.

CHAPTER
12

NICK'S INSTAGRAM MESSAGE CAME ON SUNDAY morning, not long after Quinn got home from Ivy's, when she was sitting on her bed in front of the fan, feeling the delicious breeze on her bare head. Did u mean what u said abt me seeing ur moms studio?

Anytime, Quinn wrote back.

About two seconds later she got, How's now?

Without really thinking, she wrote back, OK. 37 Cliffside.

. . . . . .

Quinn had made a terrible mistake. She realized this as soon as Nick's wheelchair turned onto her street. The houses on Cliffside were all built into the rock face. Everything was on an incline.

Quinn stood on the front steps, shading her eyes from the glare. It took a long time, but Nick finally started pushing up the driveway.

"Hey!" Quinn called from the top step.

Nick raised a hand in greeting. He pushed some more. When he reached the stone path, Quinn jogged down to meet him. Sweat wasn't just trickling down his face; it was gushing. His hair was blue-black in the sun. His shirt was green, with the words *LEAVE IT ALL ON THE TURF* in block letters on the front.

"I am so sorry," she said. "I thought you'd be getting dropped off. I thought . . ." She turned, looking hopelessly at the steep slate steps leading up to the house. "I didn't think this through."

Nick nodded, catching his breath.

"Did you bring your prosthetics?" It was a stupid question, Quinn realized. How would he carry them, in his lap? "Sorry," she said. "That was dumb . . . How do you get in your house?"

"Ramp."

"How do you get to your room?"

"Don't." He took another gulp of air. "Been sleeping downstairs. The den."

"Right." Quinn nodded. She glanced at the steps again, then back at Nick. "Well. This is nothing we can't handle."

"You . . . are not . . . piggybacking me."

"I wasn't going to piggyback you. I was thinking I'd go

get my dad. Between the two of us, I'm sure we could lift you and your chair."

Nick shook his head.

"Do you have another idea?"

He shook his head again.

"Listen," Quinn said. "I know this is weird. But I don't want you to be embarrassed. Not in front of me. Not about your legs."

Nick looked at her and said nothing.

Quinn took this as a sign to continue. "My parents are really nice. I told them you were coming. They'll be happy to help. Believe me . . . they've dealt with much weirder things."

"Are you calling me weird again?"

Quinn smiled. "Of course not."

And Nick said, "Okay."

. . . . .

It took all three of them, and they had to try a few different carrying techniques, but Quinn and her parents finally managed to get Nick and his wheelchair up to the house without much trouble. Everyone acted normal. Quinn's dad offered Nick a Coke. Quinn's mom made space at the kitchen table so Nick's chair would fit. Then she said, "Let me get Julius. He'll want to meet you, too."

"Mom," Quinn said. "Nick came to see the studio."

"This won't take long."

A minute later, Julius shuffled into the kitchen, wiggling his fingers. He stood facing the refrigerator.

"Julius," Quinn's mom said. "There's someone I'd like you to meet. This is Quinn's friend, Nick. Can you say hello to Nick?"

"Hello to Nick," Julius said in his robot voice. He wasn't even looking at Nick. His eyes were darting all over the place. His fingers were flying through the air like he was conducting an orchestra.

"Nice to meet you, Julius," Nick said. He rolled over and stuck out his hand, which of course Julius ignored.

"Julius," Quinn's mom said. "Can you look Nick in the eye?"

"Wheels, Mo. Wheels."

Quinn wanted to die, right there in the kitchen.

"That's right, bud," Quinn's mom said. "Nick's chair has wheels. Isn't it cool? I'll bet he can go really fast."

"The fastest speed ever reached by a vehicle powered through its wheels was seven hundred thirty-seven point seven nine four kilometers per hour, by the turbine-powered *Turbinator*, driven by Don Vesco, USA, at Bonneville Salt Flats, Utah, USA, on eighteen October two thousand and one."

"Oh my God," Quinn said. "Mom."

"Let him finish, honey."

"The largest Ferris wheel indoors measures forty-seven

point six zero meters. It was presented and measured in Ashgabat, Turkmenistan, on thirty April two thousand and twelve. The Ferris wheel has twenty-four cabins. The structure cost approximately ninety million dollars—"

"Mom."

"Okay." Quinn's mom nodded. "Okay."

"Wheels, Mo. Wheels." Julius was snapping his fingers like a jazz musician.

"Hey, Jules," Quinn's dad said, sweeping across the room with a tray. "I've got snacks here. What do you say we go watch some TV?"

. . . . .

"I am so sorry," Quinn said, when she and Nick finally made it out of the kitchen and into the back hall. "My brother . . . he just says whatever pops into his mouth. With no regard."

"It's not your fault," Nick said.

"I know, but still."

"Can I ask you something?"

"Yeah."

"Is he one of those child geniuses?"

Quinn shook her head. "No. He just reads the same books over and over, until it's all stuck in his brain . . . *Largest indoor Ferris wheel*. God. I am so sorry about that."

"Hey," Nick said, stopping Quinn before she could open the door to Mo's studio. "Can we make a rule?"

"What kind of rule?"

"No more apologizing."

"Okay."

"Next person who says 'I'm sorry' has to do ten push-ups."

"Really?"

"What—you don't think I can do push-ups?"

"That's not what I meant," Quinn said.

"I tried, you know. Last night, after you left. I was just lying on the couch, staring at the ceiling, and I started thinking, 'I wonder if I can still do a push-up?'"

"Could you?"

"Yeah." Nick lifted his chin a little. "I could do twelve."

Quinn was about to ask a riskier question—*Did you do them with or without your prosthetic legs?*—when her mom decided to show up.

"Thanks for waiting. It took me a while to get Julius settled." Mo looked at Nick and smiled. "Ready to see a real sculpting studio?"

Nick nodded.

"Prepare yourself," Quinn said. "It's a mess."

"Behind every great mess is a creative mind," Mo said. She twisted the handles of the French doors and pushed.

Quinn waited for Nick to roll through first. He didn't say anything for a minute. He just sat there in the middle of the room, taking it all in.

Quinn tried to imagine seeing Mo's studio for the first time. The tables covered in drop cloths and shards of clay. The spray bottles and modeling tools and aperture wire scattered everywhere. The study casts and anatomy posters. The bricks of clay wrapped in plastic, stacked against the wall. And, of course, the shelves of heads and busts in various stages of completion.

"You made all these?" Nick said, rolling over to one of the shelves.

"I did," Quinn's mom said.

Nick was leaning in, studying each piece, taking his time before moving on to the next. Quinn noticed that Julius's Sharpie hair scribbles had all disappeared. She wondered how Mo had done it. Had she used some kind of ink remover? Had she glazed over them? Quinn thought about telling Nick the story. It was pretty funny. But she stopped herself because to raise the subject of hair, even scribbled-on Sharpie hair, was to open a can of worms she definitely did not want to open. So she just stood there, watching Nick roll from shelf to shelf.

"This one's my favorite," he said finally. He'd stopped in front of Grandpa Joe. Quinn liked that one, too. The folds in the cheeks, the wrinkles around the eyes, the droopy ears and corded neck.

"That's my grandfather," Quinn said.

"Really?"

"Yeah. My mom's dad. He modeled for her a few weeks before he died."

"I'm sorry."

Quinn smiled. She held up both hands and waggled her fingers.

"What?" Nick said.

"Ten push-ups."

He let out a little groan.

"In-joke," Quinn told her mom, who looked confused. To Nick she said quickly, "You don't have to do them now. The floor's really dirty. You can do them at home. You know, honor system."

"Right."

Quinn focused her attention on a shaft of light coming through one of the windows, dust mites and clay particles suspended in the air.

"So, Nick," Quinn's mom said, breaking the silence. "Have you done much sculpting?"

"Not unless you count clay animals in second grade."

"You want to give it a try?"

"What, now?"

"Sure. Let's make you a work space." Mo shoved some stuff into a box to make room at one of the tables.

Nick rolled over.

"For a first-time sculptor," Mo said, "you'll probably find it easier to build off a base." She glanced around. "Where did I . . . ?" She strode across the room to a wooden trunk, opened it, and said, "Ah." She held up a foam head, just like the ones upstairs on Quinn's dresser. "Q?" Mo turned to Quinn. "You want to make one, too?"

"I'm good," Quinn said. "I'll just watch."

As it turned out, Nick was not a natural sculptor. Watching him slap chunks of clay onto his foam head wasn't nearly as interesting as hearing him talk while he did it.

"When we first moved here"—*slap, slap*—"my mom used to take me into Boston to visit the Museum of Fine Arts."

"She sounds like my kind of woman," Mo said. She was bent over her own work, chiseling gently.

"Yeah," Nick said. He dipped a sponge in water and squeezed way too much over a chunk of clay. "After we looked at all the art, she would take me to the museum store and let me pick out postcards. When we got home, I'd try to re-create them. I had this little box of charcoal pencils . . . But then my dad caught on, and that was the end of that."

"What happened?" Mo asked.

"He said I'd never be a professional football player if I spent all my time inside, doing my little drawings."

"How old were you?"

"I don't know. Six."

Mo actually sat speechless for a few seconds. Finally she said, "It can be difficult for nonartists to understand the artistic impulse. Remind me before you leave. I have a great book for you."

141

. . . . .

"Your mom's cool," Nick said later, when Quinn was skate-boarding beside him down Cliffside Road.

"Thanks," Quinn said.

"Your dad's cool, too."

This, Quinn knew, was not true. Her dad was anything but cool. But she was grateful to him. Phil had helped carry Nick's chair up and down the steps. He'd kept Julius out of Mo's studio. He'd even offered to drive Nick home, but Nick had said no thanks; going downhill would be way easier than going up.

"You okay there?" Quinn said when Nick's wheelchair picked up speed. She popped her board up into her hand and jogged instead, ready to reach out and grab Nick if she had to, if he lost control, if a car backed out of a driveway.

"I've got brakes," Nick said.

"Yeah, but you're not using them."

"So?"

The wheelchair sped up. Quinn ran faster. She was start-ing to feel panicky, not just at the thought of Nick flying out of his chair, but at the thought of Guinevere flying off her head. She'd done a rush job with the wig tape this morning.

"If you fall," Quinn said as she sprinted, "don't stick out your arms. Try to land on your side. And cover your face!" These were lessons she had learned the hard way when she first started riding a skateboard.

Nick let out a war whoop as he skidded to a wobbly stop at the bottom of the hill.

"Are you kidding me?" Quinn said. Her heart was pounding so hard.

"What?"

"I can't believe you didn't fall out."

"It's all about shifting your weight. Physics."

Quinn shook her head. She could feel Guinevere holding on. Whether she was 100 percent straight or not Quinn couldn't tell without a mirror.

"Is that why you won't wear your legs?" she asked. "Because you like the high-octane thrills?"

"No." He pushed off again, so Quinn couldn't see his face. "I just don't see the point."

Quinn hopped on her board and rolled up beside him. "The point of walking?"

"Of pretending they're legs. You saw them. They're not *legs*. They don't even have knee joints. I'm, like, three feet tall, waddling around. I feel like an Oompa-Loompa."

Quinn was glad Nick wasn't looking at her, because the image of him with orange skin and green hair made her smile. "Can you ask for longer ones?"

"Uh-uh. It's a progression."

"So you have to master the Oompa-Loompa legs before you can move on to the Superman legs?"

"Not Superman," he said. "Steve Austin."

"What?"

"Steve Austin legs. *The Six Million Dollar Man*. You know that show?"

"No."

"Well, you should. Check it out sometime."

"Okay, I will."

Nick kept rolling.

"You have to start somewhere," Quinn said, rolling beside him. "Don't you think?"

"I guess. I don't know."

A phone pinged. They both stopped to check their pockets.

Nick frowned at his screen.

"What?" Quinn said.

"Tommy."

"What about him?"

"My parents found out about the party. Osternek's mom has been making calls."

"Really?"

"Yeah. Tommy's grounded."

"Just for going to a party?"

Nick looked at Quinn. "Not just for going to a party. For drinking. For being an idiot. Again."

"Right." She thought about the snowmobile. "It's a good thing you weren't there."

"I gotta go," Nick said.

"You want me to come with you?"

"That's okay. It's all flat from here."

"Okay."

"I'll text you later."

"How?"

"What?"

"How will you text me later if you don't have my number?"

"I guess you'll need to give it to me," Nick said.

And Quinn said, "I guess I will."

. . . . .

When Quinn got home, she texted Ivy. R we okay?

Her phone pinged right away. Yeah y?

Quinn: Nick came over today.

Ivy: Cool.

Quinn: R u sure?

Ivy: Yes.

Quinn: B/c ur friendship matters more.

Ivy: Aww thx.

Quinn: Srsly. I don't want things to b weird.

Ivy: I meant what I said. We're good.

Quinn: K. ☺☺☺

Ivy: If I start acting like that again just smack me. ☺☺☺

CHAPTER
13

NICK'S FIRST TEXTS TO QUINN WERE ABOUT TOMMY. Tommy couldn't drive for a month. Tommy couldn't use his phone. Tommy couldn't see his friends. Except for going to school and football, Tommy was grounded. He would be spending the next thirty days staring at the ceiling in his room or doing grunt work at their dad's construction site.

R u glad? Quinn texted Nick.

And he texted back, Y would I be glad?

IDK. B/c u want him to be punished?

Nick took a while to respond. When he did, his answer surprised Quinn with its honesty. Maybe a little.

Quinn's next question, although Nick might have thought it was random, was not, in her mind, a subject change. Meet me @ the beach tmrw AM? We can walk to school.

Nick: Walk?

Quinn: Or roll. Ur call.

Nick: OK.

Quinn: OK which?

Nick: OK I will c u @ the beach tmrw.

Quinn didn't push it. She texted a thumbs-up.

. . . . .

Later that night, when she was almost asleep, Nick pinged her again. OldSkool TV. 11:30 PM.

Quinn: Y r u still awake?

Nick: Y r u?

Quinn: I was almost asleep.

Nick: Turn on ur TV.

Quinn: Y?

Nick: That show I told u about. Its on in 5 min.

Quinn: Srsly?

Nick: Yes.

Quinn: Can't I just youtube from bed?

Nick: No. We have to go old school, at the same time, so we can text while we watch.

Quinn was tired, but she tiptoed downstairs in the pitch-black and turned on the TV.

Quinn: Idk if we get that channel. What's the #?

Nick: 88.

Quinn punched two eights into the remote and got a *Beachbody* infomercial.

Quinn: U want me to watch Beachbodies?

Nick: Wait.

Quinn waited. She watched some orangey tan women in short-shorts do butt crunches. They looked strangely happy about it. Then the ad finished and a man in a space helmet filled the screen.

Nick: R u watching?

Quinn: Yes.

She was watching. After the space man's rocket malfunctioned and he crashed into the ocean, there was a corny voice-over. *Steve Austin, astronaut. A man barely alive. Gentlemen, we can rebuild him.* There were X-rays and body scans and doctors with scalpels installing the space man's new robot legs, new robot arm, and new robot eyeball, until suddenly, there he was, running down the street in a red sweat suit to the world's cheesiest soundtrack.

Quinn: Wow. She had no other words.

Nick: Keep watching. It gets better.

Quinn kept watching as Steve Austin adapted to his new abilities by running very fast, rescuing children, and punching through walls like a boss. Quinn discovered that his robot eye not only had infrared capabilities, but could also zoom to a twenty-to-one ratio. Unfortunately, his bionic parts were radioactive and would stop working in extreme cold, but on warmer days, Steve Austin's robot legs could reach speeds of sixty miles per hour, and his vertical jump was insane.

Quinn: If u had legs like that, u would school me at basketball.

Nick: True dat.

Quinn: If u had chest hair like that u would get all the ladies.

Nick: I don't need all the ladies. Just one.

Quinn didn't know how to respond to that, so she texted the silly emoticon face with one eye closed and a tongue hanging out.

Nick: I didn't mean u were my lady.

Quinn: I know.

Nick: I just meant how many ladies does a guy need?

Quinn: Right.

Nick: Anyway. Now uv met steve austin.

Quinn: Yup.

Nick: I guess I will c u tmrw.

Quinn: I guess u will.

. . . . .

When Quinn rolled onto the basketball court the next morning, she didn't see Nick anywhere. I'm here, she texted. Where r u?

Not blowing u off, Nick texted back. I have a dr's appt this AM. My mom just told me.

Quinn: Phys therapy?

Nick: Yes.

Quinn: Good luck.

Nick: Thx.

Quinn: C u in study hall?

Nick texted a thumbs-up.

Quinn slid her phone into her backpack. She dribbled her basketball to the foul line and got to work.

· · · · ·

"Are you tired?" Ivy asked in PE. "You look tired."

Quinn *was* tired. She had been up until after midnight texting with Nick. But she wasn't sure she should say this to Ivy. Even though they were "good" now, Quinn didn't want to rub her friendship with Nick in Ivy's face. It was safer to say, "I'm still recovering from the sleepover."

"Me, too." Ivy lowered her voice. "And the party."

"Yeah."

The bell rang and Ivy looked around the gym. "Where are Carm and Liss?"

"I don't know."

"I didn't see them changing. Did you?"

Quinn shook her head.

Mr. Fenner blew his whistle. "Stretch it out, people!"

Quinn and Ivy bent over the mat. After a few minutes of hamstring stretching, Lissa appeared. She wasn't dressed for PE. She was wearing sparkly flip-flops and tight white jeans.

"You guys, Carm is freaking out. She needs us."

"Where is she?" Ivy said.

"Lockah room."

As soon as Mr. Fenner was looking the other way, the three of them dashed across the gym and into the locker room. They found Carmen wedged under a sink, curled up in a ball.

"Carm," Ivy said, squatting down and waddling over to Carmen. "What's going on?"

Carmen lifted her chin from her knees. Her eyes were red and puffy.

"Talk to us," Ivy said.

Carmen shook her head.

"Carm. Come on. You're scaring me."

"He told everyone," Carmen said softly.

"Who told everyone?" Quinn said. She squatted down, too. So did Lissa.

"Rob."

"Rob from the party?" Ivy said.

Carmen nodded. "My brother Marco just texted me. He said Rob's telling everyone he hooked up with some hot freshman named Carmen."

"At least he called you hot," Lissa said.

Carmen frowned. "We did not *hook up*. We just kissed. And anyway, that's not even the worst part."

"What's the worst part?" Ivy said.

Carmen shook her head. "I can't say it."

"Carm," Lissa said, putting a hand on Carmen's knee. "This is us. You can say anything."

Carmen let out a deep, shuddering breath. "I let him take a picture of me, at the party. It wasn't bad or anything. I was wearing all my clothes. But he texted it to all his friends. He texted . . . 'this girl is good to go.'"

"Carmy!" Ivy cried. She reached out and wrapped her arms around Carmen's balled-up body.

"What did your brothah do?" Lissa said.

"Punched him in the face. Obviously."

"Obviously," Ivy said.

"Is Marco suspended?" Lissa said.

"I don't know yet." Carmen sniffled. "He texted from the principal's office. He's waiting for my parents."

"Oh, Carm." Lissa wrapped her arms around both Ivy and Carmen.

Quinn stayed where she was. She felt stupid, but she had to ask. "What does that mean, 'good to go'?"

Lissa turned her head to the side, keeping her arms around Carmen. "It's like saying she's easy."

"Like next time," Ivy said, "maybe she'll take her clothes off."

Carmen, whose voice was muffled, said, "There's not going to be a next time."

"That's for sure," Ivy said.

And Lissa said, "You messed with the wrong girl, asshat."

"I'm really sorry, Carmen," Quinn said. "I know what it's like . . . well, not the 'good to go' part, but the rest of it."

Lissa and Ivy peeled themselves off Carmen. Now everyone was looking at Quinn.

For a moment, she hesitated. She wanted to tell the story, to make Carmen feel better, but she wasn't ready to tell the whole thing. So she settled on a version of the truth. "Last year, back in Boulder? I was at this Valentine's party, and we were playing Seven Minutes in Heaven. You know that game?"

Three heads nodded.

"I went in the bathroom with this kid Ethan, and basically nothing happened. I mean he tried, but I wouldn't let him. He was being kind of . . . you know . . . handsy. So I told him to back off. But then, when we came out of the bathroom, he told everyone at the party I did something I didn't do."

"What?" Ivy said.

"You don't want to know."

"Yes," Carmen said, sitting up straight. "We do."

"Involving my mouth and his . . . *you* know."

"Ew," Lissa said.

"I know."

"You *didn't*, right?" Ivy said.

"I didn't," Quinn said. "And I told everyone at the party I didn't. I said Ethan was lying. But it didn't matter because no one believed me. They all believed him."

"That's awful," Ivy said.

"It was. It ruined my whole year." Quinn turned to Carmen. "Sorry. I didn't mean to make this about me. Just . . . you're not alone, okay?"

Carmen nodded, wiping her nose on a crumpled-up paper towel she'd been holding in her lap. "Thanks, Quinn. I appreciate that."

"You're welcome."

Suddenly, the door to the locker room opened and one of the Emmas poked her head in. "Fenner told me to come get you guys. He said, and I quote, 'I'm in the mood to give out some detentions.'"

"Tell him Lissa's having a female emergency," Ivy said. "Tell him she can't find a tampon and she's wearing white jeans."

"Me?" Lissa pointed to her chest. "Why me?"

"Because you nevah have a tampon when you need one. You're always stealing mine. And you're wearing white jeans."

"That's not true."

"You're saying your jeans aren't white?"

"No, my jeans are white, but I don't—"

"You guys," Carmen said, cutting them off. "I'm fine now. You can go back to gym."

"We're not going anywhere," Ivy said. To Emma, who was standing uncertainly in the doorway, Ivy said, "I'm serious. Tell him we're searching for tampons, and if he wants to give out detention to someone for being a good friend, then he can give it to all of us."

When Nick didn't show up to study hall, Quinn sent him a text. Where r u? I'm starting to think ur avoiding me, LOL.

It took a few minutes, but Nick texted back. PT appt went long.

Quinn: Everything ok?

Nick: Yeah. Out to lunch w/ my mom. Chili's.

Quinn: Cool.

A minute passed, and then Nick texted again. This time it was a picture, dark and kind of blurry. Look what I'm wearing.

Quinn squinted at her screen. Squinted and squinted, and then it hit her. OMG, she texted. The oompa-loompas r out to lunch?

Nick: Not by choice. It's PT homework.

Quinn: How do u feel???

Nick: Idk yet.

Quinn: Not to sound cheesy but I'm proud of u.

Nick: Thx. Gtg. My mom hates texting @ the table.

Quinn: Mine too. Ttyl?

Nick: ☺

CHAPTER
14

THE FIRST CHANCE QUINN GOT, she went on her dad's computer and searched "double leg amputation." After she discovered the correct medical term, she searched "bilateral transfemoral amputation."

She found articles, blogs, photo galleries, Facebook pages, and Twitter feeds. She learned that most new amputees are overwhelmed by how difficult it is to learn to walk on prostheses. She learned that achieving stability and balance is particularly challenging, and that, even after months of hard work and physical therapy, patients can lose hope that they will ever be able to walk again. She learned that many of them, like Nick, default to wheelchair use just because it's easier. She learned that the legs Nick had left were called residual limbs. She learned that those white stocking thingies he wore were called stump socks. She learned that there was a whole "stump care regimen" that Nick had to follow so his skin wouldn't break down. She learned that the metal legs she'd seen him using at the Shoreline North Medical Center were called short prosthetics with training feet. She learned that finding a comfortable sleep position is nearly impossible. Nick couldn't sleep with his residual limbs resting on a pillow because this would shorten his hip flexors. Nick couldn't sleep with a pillow between his legs because this would lengthen the inner thigh muscles that kept his legs together and shorten the outer thigh muscles that kept his legs apart, both of which would make walking even more difficult. She learned—and this was the worst thing of all—that Nick could still feel pain in his feet and calves and knees, even though they were gone. *Phantom pain*, it was called.

Quinn didn't know what to do with any of this information. So she just sat there, staring at the computer, letting it all sink in.

"Q?"

Quinn jolted in the chair. "You scared me!"

"Sorry," her mom said. "I didn't mean to sneak up on you. I just have to grab some paper." She reached past Quinn to a stack on the desk. "What are you looking at?"

"Nothing."

Quinn tried to cover the screen, but Mo was already leaning in. " 'Spouses, family members, and friends play a significant role in helping the amputee adjust to the disability—' "

"Mom," Quinn said. "Come on."

"Are you searching for ways to help Nick?"

"I don't know. Maybe." Quinn felt her face go warm.

"Honey, that is so . . . I am so proud to have you for a daughter. Do I tell you that enough? How *proud* I am?"

Quinn rolled her eyes. "Mom. Relax."

"I'm just saying . . . Nick's lucky to have you for a friend."

"Yeah. Okay."

"Would you like to have him over for dinner some night this week? I could make lasagna."

"I don't know. Maybe."

"Well," her mom said. "Think about it. He's welcome anytime."

. . . . . .

When Quinn came downstairs later, there was a big glass jar of M&M's on the kitchen counter.

"What's this?" she said.

"That," Mo said, looking up from the onions she was chopping, "is a behavioral incentive for Julius. When he meets one of his goals, he gets a reward."

"Candy?"

"Sometimes candy, sometimes a nonfood incentive like extra TV time or a trip to the bookstore."

"So basically you're bribing him."

"We're not bribing him," Mo said, sweeping the onions into a pot. "We're offering him positive reinforcement."

158

"I thought Julius wasn't supposed to eat sugar. Or Red 40."

"He shouldn't have a lot of it, but a little—"

"Those were my concerns, too," Quinn's dad said, strolling into the kitchen with a carrot in his hand. He planted a kiss on top of Quinn's head, tickling her scalp with his beard. *"Salve, filia."*

"Hi, Dad."

"If either of you has a better idea," Mo said, turning on the stove, "have at it. But I'm the one going to Julius's team meetings at the Cove. I'm the one talking with his teachers on a daily basis. I'm the one—"

"M&M's, Mo," Julius said, shuffling into the kitchen with one hand in the air. "M&M's Monday."

"That's right, bud," Quinn's mom said, turning around and wiping her hands on a dish towel. "Today is Monday. And those are M&M's in that jar. After you wash up for dinner, you may have an M&M."

Quinn's dad opened his mouth to say something, but Mo stopped him. "Phil," she said. "Don't. You haven't been to a single one of his meetings. Until you do, just . . . don't."

"I have a job, Maureen. A job that allows Julius to go to that school and you to go to those meetings. If I don't show up for my job—"

"Too loud," Julius said, clapping his hands over his ears. "Too loud, Phil."

"Phil," Quinn's mom said quietly, shooting him a look.

Quinn's dad opened his mouth again. This time he took a bite of carrot.

. . . .

Does ur dad ever take u to PT? Quinn sent the text to Nick and then she pulled down the shades in her room. She turned out the lights. She sat on her bed and, inch by inch, she ran her fingers over her scalp. *Anything there? No. Anything there? No. Anything there—*

Her phone pinged.

Nick: Where did that come from?

Quinn: Sorry. Weird night here. Parents arguing abt whose job it is to take Julius to his appts.

Nick: Drop and give me 10.

He had her. She got down on the rug and banged out ten push-ups in the dark. Then she hopped back on her bed and texted, Bam.

Nick: My dad never takes me to PT. Just my mom.

Quinn: Y?

Nick: Not his thing.

Quinn: What's not?

Nick: IDK. Hospitals. Weakness.

Quinn: Ur not weak.

Nick: Wtv.

Quinn: Ur not. What ur going thru, learning to walk agn. That takes srs strength.

Nick texted a string of emojis she didn't recognize.

Quinn: What r those?

Nick: Cheeseballs. B/c ur being a cheeseball.

Quinn: Speaking of cheese, my mom wants to know if u want to come over for lasagna.

Nick: When?

Quinn: Whenev. Some night this wk.

Nick: OK.

Quinn scrolled back through their old texts until she found the photo Nick had sent earlier, of his Oompa-Loompa legs under the table at Chilis. She retexted the photo with a new comment. These guys r invited too.

Nick didn't respond right away, making Quinn wonder if she'd made a mistake. But finally her phone pinged. I'll think abt it.

She texted back three smiley faces, which may have been overkill, but she didn't care.

CHAPTER
15

ON TUESDAY MORNING, MO WAS STANDING at the kitchen counter. Just standing there, staring out the window at the backyard. She was wearing her flannel PJ bottoms and a green silky blouse.

Quinn stopped in the doorway. "Mom?"

Mo turned around. She was wearing one gold hoop earring. There was toothpaste in the corner of her mouth. "Hi."

"What's going on?"

Mo squeezed her eyes shut for a second. When she opened them she said, "Did you hear the phone ring in the middle of the night?"

"No. Why?"

"It was Grandma Gigi's nursing home. She fell on her way to the bathroom and broke her hip."

"Oh my God." Quinn felt her eyes prickle.

"She'll be okay. She's scheduled for surgery tomorrow morning. I need to fly to Phoenix for a few days."

"Okay." Quinn nodded slowly, processing. "Are you bringing Julius?"

"I have to."

"Right." Quinn couldn't picture Julius without Mo, even for twenty-four hours. Had she ever gone away? Quinn couldn't remember a time.

"But Julius in an airport?" Mo shook her head. "Julius on a plane all the way to Arizona?"

"Right," Quinn said. She pictured Julius melting down at 35,000 feet. She pictured mini bags of pretzels flying.

"He needs his routine," Mo said. "He's just beginning to feel settled here. This is just . . . horrible timing."

There were sounds from upstairs. Footsteps. The low rumble of voices. Now would have been a good opportunity for Quinn to say, *Don't worry about Julius, Mom. He can stay. Dad and I know what to do.* But she couldn't make the words come out.

"What about Uncle Andrew?" Quinn said. Uncle Andrew was Mo's younger brother. They never saw him.

"He's in Australia."

"Since when?"

"Since he took a teaching position at University of Sydney."

"Okay . . . ," Quinn said. Nobody ever told her anything. That much was clear.

"I've been making lists." Quinn's mom shuffled some

papers on the counter. "School times. Meals and snacks. Transitional aids. Positive reinforcements. Phone numbers for all of his teachers and therapists—"

"Wait—so you're *not* bringing Julius?"

"Yes," her mom said. "No." She shook her head so the single gold hoop earring swung. "I don't know."

Quinn thought: *My mother is having a breakdown.*

Quinn thought: *I need to say something.*

"Mom. It'll be okay."

"Will it?"

"Yes," Quinn said. Then, "Geege needs you right now."

"I know."

"If you bring Julius, you won't really be there for her."

Quinn's mom huffed out a breath. "I know."

"Leave him here," Quinn said. "He'll be fine. We know what to do."

Mo smiled a little. "That's just what your father said."

"Because it's true."

There was no reason to assume that Quinn and her dad couldn't handle the job. They'd known Julius as long as Mo had.

"Listen," Quinn said. From upstairs came Phil's deep voice singing. *You put your right foot in, you put your left foot in.* "Julius is putting on his pants. And when he comes downstairs, I will make him breakfast tacos. Because it's Tuesday." Breakfast tacos weren't hard to make. They were just scrambled eggs and bacon wrapped in little tortilla sleeping bags. "Okay?"

Quinn's mom nodded. "Okay."

"Why don't you go put on some pants?"

Mo looked at her PJ bottoms.

"And your other earring."

Mo reached up to touch her empty earlobe. "Yes." She started to walk out of the kitchen. Then she stopped in the doorway and turned around. "You and Dad can call me anytime, you know, with questions. You just won't be able to reach me when I'm on the plane." She frowned. "Maybe not at the hospital, either. In certain rooms they make you turn off your cell because the signal interferes with the medical equipment . . . but you can always leave me a message and I'll call you right back."

"Mom. We'll be fine."

"Are you sure?"

Quinn wasn't sure, but she nodded. "Yes."

Mo took a deep breath and plastered on a smile. "Thank you, honey."

"You're welcome."

. . . . . .

Quinn let her parents drive her to school. This seemed to be what Quinn's mom needed before she went to the airport. "I want to see you off properly," Mo said, which didn't sound like her. *See you off properly?* Since when had their family done anything properly? When Quinn thought of *proper*, she

165

thought of Queen Elizabeth serving crumpets from a silver-plated tea service, not Phil riding shotgun with his white-framed sunglasses from the 1980s or Mo with her messy ponytail and crooked red lipstick, shooting manic smiles in the rearview mirror. Quinn's mom never wore lipstick. Quinn had no idea why she was wearing it now.

"This is going to be an adventure," Mo said, for the fourth or fifth time. "Right, bud?"

Julius wasn't even listening. He had his headphones on. He was muttering to himself and staring out the window.

Quinn wanted to tell her mother to relax. She wanted to say, *He's fine. See? He doesn't need you as much as you think he does.* But Quinn didn't want to say anything that would make her mom act any crazier than she already was.

· · · · ·

"You can still come over," Quinn told Nick in study hall, after she'd explained about Grandma Gigi. "My mom just won't be there, so . . . you know . . . no lasagna. But we could still hang out."

"Okay."

"My dad won't get home from picking up Julius until at least four o'clock . . . just for timing purposes, with the stairs, if you need help."

"Okay."

166

"If your dad drops you off, probably the two of us could do it. Or your mom. She's used to lifting your chair, right?"

"Quinn," Nick said.

"Yeah?"

"Shut up."

Quinn nodded. "Right."

"You don't need to worry about me."

"Okay . . . are you still coming over?"

"Yes, weirdo," Nick said. "I'm still coming over."

. . . . .

When Nick's car pulled into Quinn's driveway, Quinn was already there, working on some of her skateboarding tricks. The ollie, the nollie, the no comply, and this new one she'd been trying to master called the disco flip, where you ollie and pop and kick the front foot for the heelflip. Then you turn your shoulders backside while you make the flip and continue to rotate your body. You only need to rotate ninety degrees, and you can throw your feet on the board in reverse, catch it, and roll away. Quinn was doing the roll-away when she saw Nick's car pull in. She hopped off her board and waved.

When Quinn saw Nick get out of the passenger seat on his short metal legs, she tried not to smile. She made her face completely neutral as she walked over.

"Hi, Mrs. Strout," she said, holding out her hand. "I'm Quinn."

Nick's mom had dark, wavy hair and a square jaw like Tommy's. She was shorter than Quinn by a few inches, and her hands were small, but her grip was strong. "Nice to meet you, Quinn."

"You, too."

"Wow. You can really skateboard."

"Thanks." Quinn smiled. Then she turned to Nick. "Hey."

"Hey," he said gruffly. He didn't meet Quinn's eye. She wanted to tell him not to feel self-conscious. She didn't care how short his legs were.

"Nicky," his mom said. "Do you want some help getting up those stairs?"

"No."

"Are you sure?" Mrs. Strout frowned at the slate steps. "They look pretty steep. And there's no railing."

"I've got it. You can go."

Quinn watched Nick's mom start to move in for a kiss, then hesitate, then smooch him on the head anyway.

"Mom," he said in a strangled voice.

"Sorry," his mom said. "Bye, honey. Bye, Quinn."

"Bye, Mrs. Strout."

· · · · · · ·

Watching Nick navigate the front steps was like watching one of those puppets on strings. Because his prosthetics had no knee joints, he had to lean all the way to one side to lift the

168

opposite leg onto the next step. Then he had to stand straight up and balance on one metal foot before leaning all the way to the *other* side and lifting the opposite leg up. It looked really hard. It took forever. Quinn wanted to cheer him on, to offer words of encouragement each time he scaled another step, but she knew Nick well enough by now to keep her mouth shut. The only time she opened it was when he got to the top, and then she said, "You want a Coke?"

. . . . .

Julius didn't exactly ruin everything, but he didn't help, either. Maybe ten minutes after Quinn got Nick's Coke, Julius pounded on the front door. As soon as Quinn opened it and heard him muttering, "Mo. Mo makes my snack. *Mo* makes my snack," she knew.

"Rough day?" she said to her dad.

He was trailing behind Julius, *Guinness World Records 2017* in one hand and yellow headphones in the other. His glasses were smudged and there was a blotchy red stain on his white shirt. "You have no idea."

"Hi, Julius," Quinn said, even though she knew it was pointless. "How was school today?"

"Mo picks me up," Julius said quietly to the coatrack. "Mo." He paused to do one of his rock-and-roll moves, shifting his weight forward and backward, snapping his fingers high in the air. "Mo picks me up."

"Right," Quinn said, turning back to her father. "So, Dad, Nick's here. He's in the bathroom right now, but I just wanted to let you know, before he comes out—"

"Legs," Julius said, not quietly. "Legs. Legs. Legs."

Quinn swore under her breath. She tried to catch Nick's eye to tell him she was sorry, but he wasn't looking at her. He was standing in the doorway, watching her brother.

"Hi, Nick." Quinn's dad tucked the book under his elbow and walked briskly past Julius to shake Nick's hand. "Nice to see you again."

"Svetlana Pankratova of Russia has the world's longest legs—"

Of course, Quinn thought. Of course this was happening right now. She closed her eyes.

"—verified as measuring one hundred and thirty-two centimeters, fifty-one point nine inches, in Torremolinos, Spain, on eight July two thousand and three."

"I'm very sorry," Quinn's dad murmured. "He's a little thrown off by his mother being out of town."

Quinn opened her eyes to shoot her dad a look, but he was focused on Julius. "Bud, you remember Nick? Can you say hello?"

Snap, flap, kick. The triple threat.

Nick took a few halting steps forward. "Hi, Julius."

"Wheels."

Oh dear Lord. If Quinn could have grabbed Nick under

170

her arm like a football and run him out of the house, she would have.

"That's right," Nick said to Julius. "The last time you saw me I had my wheels. This time I have my legs."

Julius stopped moving for about a nanosecond. "They're short."

"Yeah," Nick said. "They are. Because they don't have knees."

"Largest game of head, shoulders, knees, and toes . . ."

If Quinn's dad hadn't been there as a witness, Quinn might not have believed what she was hearing herself. Julius and Nick were having a conversation. Kind of. And the only people Julius had conversations with were Mo, Phil, and Q.

. . . . .

"What are you making?" Quinn asked her dad later. Julius was watching TV. Nick was in Mo's studio, putting the finishing touches on his sculpture's nose, which didn't look half bad.

"Pizza," her dad said. He was standing at the kitchen counter, rolling out dough.

"Seriously?" Quinn said.

Her dad grinned. He had flour on his nose. "When you were little, we used to make pizza together every Friday night. Do you remember?"

Quinn shook her head. "It's Tuesday."

"We can pretend it's Friday."

"Hello? Taco Tuesday?" Quinn walked over to the refrigerator, where her mom had tacked up all her instructions. Quinn tapped the meal plan with her finger. " 'Tuesday dinner. Tacos. Ground beef in the fridge. Chop the tomatoes as small as possible. Use the tomatillo salsa . . .' Did you even read this?"

"I read it. And I decided to make pizza."

"Dad," Quinn said. "Mom wrote this down for a reason. She knows what she's doing."

"So do I," Quinn's dad said, slopping a spoonful of sauce onto his rolled-out dough. "Tonight we're trying something new. Phil's rules."

Quinn stared at him. "Phil's rules?"

"Phil's rules," he repeated, smoothing the sauce with the back of his spoon.

"You're going rogue."

"I'm expanding your brother's culinary horizons."

"Just for the record," Quinn said, "I think you're making a mistake."

"Maybe."

"Julius is going to flip out."

"Possibly. Let's see what happens."

. . . . .

172

What happened was hand flapping and finger snapping and foot kicking and ear smacking and "Taco Tuesday, Phil, Taco Tuesday, Taco Tuesday, Phil, Phil, Taco Tuesday, Phil, Taco Tuesday, Phil," until finally, Julius grabbed the freshly baked pizza off the stovetop and flung it across the kitchen like a discus, splattering sauce and cheese everywhere.

Quinn's dad stared at the mess.

Quinn stared at her dad.

Julius smacked his ears.

"You know," Nick said, "there's a Mexican place in town that delivers. La Cucaracha. They make really good tacos."

Quinn's dad turned to Nick and said, *"Deus te benedicat."*

Nick looked at Quinn.

"It's Latin," she said. "He just blessed you."

. . . . .

"So," Quinn said, when she and Nick were standing out on the front lawn, waiting for Nick's mom to pick him up. "Have we scared you away forever?"

"I don't scare that easy," Nick said.

"You don't?"

"Nah. You should see some of the blowouts at my house when all my brothers are home. One Thanksgiving, Kip threw the vacuum across the dining room at Gavin. It landed on the turkey."

Quinn laughed. "Really?"

"Yeah. My mom was so mad."

It was still a little unreal to Quinn that Nick was standing here on her front lawn. Literally standing. Going down the stairs had been tricky. A few times Quinn had almost reached out to grab his arm, but it turned out she didn't have to.

"Speak of the devil," Nick said as his mom's car pulled into the driveway. He started walking, slow, wobbly steps down the path.

"Hey," Quinn said, walking behind him. "Thanks for suggesting that Mexican place. The tacos were really good."

"I know, right?"

"I liked the hot sauce," Quinn said. "And I don't usually like hot sauce."

"I like you," Nick said.

At least that was what Quinn *thought* he said. That was what it sounded like. But he was facing the other direction, and his mom's car was running, so it was kind of hard to hear.

"What?" she said.

But Nick was already getting into the front seat, saying something to his mom. Now he was waving goodbye to Quinn, a regular wave, not an I-like-you sort of wave. So probably what he'd said was *I like juice*, which was what they'd had to drink with their tacos. Grape juice.

Yeah, Quinn thought, as she waved back. *I like juice.* That made more sense.

CHAPTER
16

THURSDAY WAS AN EARLY DISMISSAL. Professional development for teachers and no after-school activities. "You should come to JB's with us," Ivy said to Quinn during PE. "It's tradition."

"Yeah," Carmen said, "we stuff ourselves with mozzarella sticks and Lissa barfs in the trash can."

"That only happened once," Lissa said.

"Yes. But it was legendary."

"I can't," Quinn said.

"What?" Ivy said. "You have coolah friends to hang out with?"

Quinn shook her head. "My mom's out of town, remember? I have to help my dad."

"With what?" Carmen said.

"My brother."

"How old is he again?" Lissa said.

"Nine."

She could have left it there. All her friends knew was that Quinn had a nine-year-old brother, so they probably assumed he went to one of the elementary schools in town and had an early dismissal, too. But not saying more, not being completely honest, was beginning to feel like a heavy box Quinn had been lugging around. She was tired of carrying it, so she set it down and let something crawl out. "He has autism. He goes to the Cove. He doesn't have early dismissal, but he's had a hard time since my mom left, and my dad is, like, flailing, so I want to be home in case his school calls and we have to go get him."

Quinn waited for awkward silence to set in. But Lissa said, "I get it. My sistah has Down syndrome."

"She does?" Quinn said.

"Uh-huh. Not my oldah sistah, Jenny. My youngah sistah, Mae. She's mainstreamed at the middle school."

"We love Mae," Ivy said.

And Carmen said, "Mae is the bomb. She gives the best hugs."

"Well," Quinn said, trying not to look surprised. "I hope I get to meet her sometime."

. . . . .

Quinn texted her dad as she was walking home. On my way. I can help w/ J's snacks and dinner. Thermos Thurs.

176

Then Quinn sent a quick group text to the girls. Sry to miss JBs. Eat a mozz stick for me.

Finally, she sent a text to Nick, who she hadn't seen all day because there was no lunch or study hall. Hey. Hope ur doing something fun w/ ur free afternoon. Check in l8r.

When Quinn got to her house and unlocked the front door, there was a piece of notebook paper taped to the floor in the foyer. *Salve, filia. I'm heading to town in search of cappuccino and a quiet spot to grade papers. Home by 4:00 with the divine Julius in tow. Love, Dad.*

Huh. Quinn thought for a minute. She could still go into town and meet the girls. She could hop on her skateboard and be there in twenty minutes.

Or.

Quinn reached up and peeled Guinevere off her head. *Rip, rip, rip*, went the wig tape.

This feeling. This, right here. It was like diving into a pool on a hundred-degree day. It was like finally getting to pee after holding it for hours.

Quinn gave her scalp a good, long scratch. She walked into the kitchen and got herself a bag of chips, a bowl of baby carrots. She carried her snacks into the living room and kicked her feet up on the coffee table. She clicked on the TV.

There was nothing to watch. Game shows. Soap operas in English. Soap operas in Spanish. More game shows. Quinn flipped from channel to channel until she came upon three women sitting in a row with hair salon capes over their shoulders. One by one, the trio of stylists standing behind them held up signs. *Choose a cut that flatters your face. Consider your color. Take stock of your styling products.* It was the kind of stupid show that Quinn would normally never watch. She would skip right over it. But today, she stayed where she was. She sat on the couch, and she ate her snacks, and she watched the three women get transformed. Long hair to pixie cut. Bleached blond to honey brown. All-one-length to shaggy, chunky layers. She watched the women squeal and shriek and thank their stylists for changing their looks, for changing their lives.

When the show was over, Quinn clicked off the TV. She walked into her dad's office. She sat down at his computer and logged on to the alopeciasucks.com message board.

FuzzyWuzzy: Anyone out there? I need to vent.

It didn't take long for a response to pop up.

BaldFacedTruth: I'm here Fuzz. You ok?

Quinn took a breath. She started to type.

FuzzyWuzzy: I hate my wig. I HATE my wig. HATE IT. Every time I take it off I am so relieved I want to set it on fire so I never have to wear it again. But I am also grateful for it because for the past month it has transformed me. I know that sounds dramatic but it's actually how it feels, like I've morphed into someone else. Which is what I thought I needed. Did u see my old post that I started at a new school? And that no one here knows I am AAT?

BaldFacedTruth: I have been following all ur posts. How was the sleepover?

FuzzyWuzzy: Fine. I mean my wig stayed on all night and no one could tell, but it sucked too b/c I was nervous the whole time and I felt like I was being sneaky, u know? That's how I have felt this whole time, like I am not being honest w my new friends. Meanwhile, some of them have been very honest w me abt personal things with them that I have not judged them on. But I am still afraid to tell them.

BaldFacedTruth: What do u think will happen if u do?

FuzzyWuzzy: Idk.

BaldFacedTruth: Do u trust them?

FuzzyWuzzy: I think so. But I trusted my old friends too, and that was a mistake.

BaldFacedTruth: What happened?

FuzzyWuzzy: Long story.

BaldFacedTruth: Ive got time.

So Quinn started at the beginning. She began with the first time she told Paige and Tara about her alopecia. She wrote about how they tried to act normal, but Quinn could tell they thought it was weird. How they were always trying to get her to wear something other than her Colorado Rockies baseball cap. How, before the Valentine's party, they took Quinn to

179

Anthropologie and insisted that she buy the red-and-white beanie with the earflaps.

Quinn kept writing and writing. She wrote about that One Stupid Night. She wrote about what happened in Paige's bathroom. She wrote about Ethan lying to everyone, and laughing, and stuffing his face with the cookies she'd baked. She wrote about the Monday after the party. The girls on her basketball team cornering her in the locker room. The picture Sammy Albee had posted on Instagram, with its horrible caption. Quinn kept writing until she heard the front door bang open and a pounding of footsteps in the hall.

"Q? I need your help!"

Quinn stood up. "Dad?"

She found her father in the kitchen, gathering random items. A bag of Goldfish crackers. A spoon. Napkins.

"What are you doing?" Quinn said. "What's wrong?"

Her dad dropped a warm hand onto Quinn's head, just for a moment. "Hi. Everything's fine. I just forgot I have a department dinner. I have to drive into the city in, oh"—he glanced at his watch—"ten minutes if I'm going to make it. You'll be okay for a few more hours, right? Can you help me find some of your brother's things? His favorite books? The blue iPod? It has that playlist he likes, *Indigo Dreams*."

"You're bringing Julius to your department dinner?"

"I have to." Her dad opened a drawer, pulled out a handful of plastic straws. "It's mandatory . . . Honey, I really need that iPod—"

"Didn't you tell them about Grandma Gigi? I thought you were taking personal days."

"I am." Quinn's dad shoved the straws and the Goldfish crackers and the spoon into his briefcase. "But this is too important. The dean of the faculty will be there. If I want any chance of renewing my contract for next year . . . Q." He looked at her with pleading eyes. "The blue iPod. Can you look?"

Quinn stared back at him. "You've got to be kidding."

"What?"

"You can't bring Julius to a department dinner with the dean of the faculty. That's, like, the worst idea in the history of ideas."

"What choice do I have?"

"Leave him here. With me."

Her dad shook his head. "I can't do that."

"Why not? I'm fourteen. I've been babysitting the Lindt twins since I was twelve." It was true. Back in Colorado, Quinn used to babysit Thomas and James at least once a week.

Quinn's dad shook his head again. "Julius isn't the Lindt twins."

"No kidding. He's my brother. You don't think I know how to babysit my own brother?"

Her dad glanced at his watch. "I don't know, Quinn."

"Dad," she said. She pointed at the refrigerator, at the six pieces of paper stuck on with magnets. "Mom wrote everything down. It's right there. All his foods. All his routines. Go pick up Julius and bring him back here. I'll get his snack ready."

"He's in the car," Quinn's dad said.

"What?"

"I already went to the Cove. He's waiting outside in the car."

"You left him outside?"

"Just for a few minutes. I locked the doors."

"You *locked him in the car*?"

"He's fine. He's watching something on my phone. The world's fastest tortoise."

Quinn stared at her father. For such a smart guy, he was acting really dumb. "Give me your keys," she said. "And go put on some dinner clothes."

Quinn's dad glanced down at the faded Bon Jovi concert shirt and ripped jeans he'd been wearing since the morning. "Good point."

When Quinn got outside, she expected to find Julius melting down inside her dad's car. She expected him to be screaming, pounding the windows with his face. But he was just sitting there in the backseat, headphones on, bent over her dad's phone, watching a YouTube video about the world's fastest tortoise. Her dad was right. Julius was fine.

Slowly and quietly, Quinn slid across the backseat. "Hi, bud," she said. She picked up his lunch box. "What do you say you unstrap your seat belt and come inside with me? I'll make you a snack."

"It's thermos Thursday, Q," her brother said, not looking up from the tortoise.

"That's right," Quinn said. "It's thermos Thursday. How do you feel about oatmeal?"

"I feel good about oatmeal."

"Good," Quinn said. "That's what I'll make."

She had this, she thought. Easy peasy.

. . . . . .

Quinn wasn't sure how it happened, exactly. One minute Julius was parked in front of the TV with his thermos of oatmeal, his three perfectly smooth blankets, and his VHS recording of *Guinness World Records Primetime*. The next minute he was gone.

Gone.

What had happened was this: Quinn was in the kitchen, chopping onions. Chili was what her mom had recommended for Thursday's dinner. It was a win-win: Julius liked chili, and chili fit in a thermos. The recipe was right there on the fridge. So Quinn was chopping away when her phone pinged. It was a Snapchat from Ivy, Carmen, and Lissa. Their mouths were open and they were barfing up rainbows. The caption read, *We ate too much.*

Quinn snapped back a picture of the onion she was chopping. *I'm making dinner.*

Ivy snapped back a picture of herself wearing hippie glasses and a flower tiara, holding her fingers in a V. *Peace.*

Quinn almost snapped a picture of herself with bunny

ears and a pink nose, but then it hit her: Holy crap. She wasn't wearing her wig. She ran to the foyer and grabbed Guinevere off the table, not bothering with wig tape, just stopping in front of the hall mirror to make sure her part was straight.

Back in the kitchen, Quinn tried again. Rabbit ears. Pink nose. *Somebunny loves u.*

Carmen snapped back a picture of her and Lissa with huge, stretched-out mouths and tiny piggy eyes.

Quinn snapped back a picture of her face beside the pan of sautéing onions and browning meat. *Chillin w my chili.*

This went on for some time. She dumped a can of pinto beans on top of the meat, snapped a picture. Quinn dumped a can of diced tomatoes on top of the beans, snapped a picture. When the simmering time was up, she put down her phone. She scooped chili into a thermos and set it on the table with a spoon and thermos top of milk. She walked into the living room to tell Julius dinner was ready.

Julius wasn't there.

Quinn looked around the room. The TV was off. The blankets were on the floor.

"Jules?" she said, not too loudly. "Where are you, bud?"

No answer.

She checked the downstairs bathroom. No Julius. She checked the laundry room. No Julius. She checked Phil's office. No Julius.

"Buddy? Dinner's ready."

Quinn wasn't worried yet. Not really. Julius had probably

184

gone up to his room, to find one of his books or to lie under his weighted blanket for a while, staring at the ceiling. He did that sometimes after school, to decompress.

"Julius?"

His room was empty. So was the upstairs bathroom. So was Quinn's room, and her parents' room, and the tiny spare bedroom filled with baskets of laundry waiting to be folded.

"Bud?"

Quinn could hear her voice getting louder. She could feel a tightening in her chest as she ran back downstairs to check Mo's studio. *You don't think I know how to babysit my own brother?* she'd told her dad.

Julius wasn't in Mo's studio.

He wasn't in the front yard.

He wasn't in the backyard.

"Julius!"

Quinn's chest was getting tighter and tighter. What was she supposed to do, call her dad and interrupt his department dinner? Call her mom, 2,600 miles away, and send her into a panic by saying *I can't find Julius?* No way was she doing that. No freaking way.

Quinn had lost her brother. He had vanished, right under her nose. How could this have happened?

Quinn ran back into the kitchen and grabbed her phone off the counter. Her hands were literally shaking as she called the first person she could think of.

"Nick?" she said. "I need help."

. . . . .

Fifteen minutes later, Tommy's piece-of-junk car pulled into Quinn's driveway. She ran down the front steps.

"Hey—" she said when Tommy hopped out of the car. He was wearing a tight black T-shirt and Gulls Head football shorts. "Aren't you still grounded?"

"Yup," Tommy said.

"But—you're allowed to drive?"

"Nope," Tommy said.

Quinn turned to Nick, who was easing his legs out of the backseat and onto the pavement. "I thought when you said someone would drive you, you meant your mom or dad."

"My mom's getting her hair cut," Nick said. "My dad's at work. You said right away."

"Yeah, but . . . I don't want Tommy to get in *more* trouble."

"Hey," Tommy said. "Let me worry about that." He put his hand on Quinn's shoulder. "What can I do to help?"

For a second, Quinn just looked at him. Tommy Strout was the nicest person in the world. How could Nick hate him so much?

"What do you need?" Tommy said.

The tightness in Quinn's chest returned full force. "I can't find my brother. He just . . . took off."

CHAPTER
17

IT DIDN'T REGISTER WITH QUINN UNTIL she and Tommy were halfway up the slate steps and Nick was hobbling behind them. "Oh my God," she said when it hit her. She hadn't seen Nick all day. She turned around and looked at him. "Did you wear your legs to school?"

"No. I put them on when I got home, to practice stairs."

Tommy turned around, too. "Hop on my back," he said.

"I'm not getting on your back," Nick said.

"Nicky. It's steep. Hop on."

"No."

"Nick," Tommy said.

And Quinn said, "Shhh."

She heard Julius before she saw him, his voice floating down from somewhere high. "We have been recording the world's achievements since 1955. Yours could be next."

Sure enough, when she looked up—one, two, three stories, to the very top of her house—Quinn saw her brother. Blue sweatpants. Red shirt. Blond stegosaurus hair, lit up by the sun that was just starting to set.

Julius was on the roof.

Julius was on the roof, and he was snapping his fingers.

OhmyGodohmyGodohmyGod, Quinn thought.

"Is that him?" Tommy said.

Quinn nodded. She wanted to scream through cupped hands, *What are you doing? Get off the roof!* But you couldn't scream at Julius.

"Come on," Quinn said.

She launched herself up the steps, two at a time. She flung open the front door. She sprinted up the stairs to the second floor, through her parents' bedroom, over to the ceiling panel with the fold-down ladder. It hadn't occurred to Quinn to check the attic. It wasn't a finished room. It was full of mouse droppings and loose insulation and cardboard boxes that her parents still hadn't unpacked. Quinn had only been up to the attic once, but she remembered another fold-down ladder that led outside. Her dad had gone up there to fix a gutter.

"Roof access?" Tommy said. He was right behind Quinn.

"Yeah." She started to climb. "You need to know something before we get up there. My brother doesn't like loud noises. And he hates to be touched."

"Okay," Tommy said.

"But if we have to grab him, we grab him."

188

"Right," Tommy said. "We won't let him fall."

Quinn and Tommy made their way through the mess to the ladder leading straight up to a skylight in the roof.

That was when Quinn suddenly remembered how much she hated heights. Hated them. The nausea she felt when she climbed the narrow wooden slats and stepped out through the skylight reminded her that nothing—not a bald head, not Ethan Hess, not an itchy wig that she'd thrown on so hastily it could come off in the next stiff breeze—nothing was worse than standing on the roof of a three-story house. Especially not a roof that her brother—her orchestra-conducting, jazz-finger-snapping, tap-dancing, judo-kicking brother—was currently on top of.

Standing on the roof, taking fast, panicky gulps of air, Quinn thought for a moment that she would pass out.

"Maybe you should go first," Tommy whispered.

Yes. Quinn nodded.

What would Mo do? This was the question Quinn asked herself as she inched her way forward. Mo would use her calmest voice, her slowest movements.

"Julius?" Quinn spoke softly. She crept slowly. "Hey, bud. It's Q."

"Q." Julius didn't turn around, but he snapped his fingers excitedly.

"That's right." Quinn took another baby step forward. Her knees were shaking, but her voice held steady. "What are we doing up here?"

189

"On twenty-one April two thousand fourteen, Fred Fugen and Vince Reffet, both from France, broke the Guinness World Record for highest BASE jump from a building with a jump of eight hundred twenty-eight meters, two thousand seven hundred and sixteen feet, six inches. They performed the jump off the Burj Khalifa tower in Dubai, UAE."

"Wow," Quinn said. Another shuffle forward. "That's really high."

"I'm the highest BASE jump kid," Julius said, snapping away.

"What's that, bud?"

"I'm the highest BASE jump kid, Q. The highest BASE jump kid."

Quinn's stomach dropped, either from the view of the ground, which she could now see looming below her, or from the words coming out of her brother's mouth. Quinn forced her eyes to look straight ahead. She breathed through her nose. "You want to break the world record for BASE jumping?"

"Not break a record. Set a record. I'm the highest BASE jump kid."

Holy shiz. Holyshizholyshizholyshiz.

Quinn took another breath.

"Buddy," she said softly. "Those guys who BASE jump? They wear special stuff. Like helmets. And parachutes. And . . . you know . . . kneepads. Like the ones I wear sometimes when I'm skateboarding."

190

"Kneepads." Julius gave a little kick that took him closer to the edge.

"That's right. And you're not wearing kneepads right now, are you?"

"I'm wearing sweatpants, Q. Size ten."

"Right." Quinn shuffled forward another centimeter. "And sweatpants, bud? Sweatpants are *not* what you want to wear to set the first kid's BASE jumping record. They're not thick enough. They won't protect your knees."

"They won't protect your knees."

"That's right. Only kneepads will protect your knees . . . Hey, bud. Why don't you take my hand and we'll go downstairs and find you some kneepads?"

"No touching, Q. I don't like touching."

"Yeah, I know you don't like touching. But it'll just be for a minute, until we get to the ladder, okay?"

"A minute is sixty seconds."

"That's right. It probably won't even take that long. It'll be more like twenty seconds. Okay?"

"Okay, Q."

Quinn reached out her hand. Julius did one of his spontaneous spin moves, catching his heel on one of the roof shingles. Tommy and Quinn dove at the same time. Tommy's hand grabbed her brother's shirt. Julius's hand grabbed Quinn's hair. The three of them landed on the roof in a series of slow-motion thumps.

Quinn . . .

Julius . . .

Tommy . . .

Guinevere didn't land with a thump. She made no sound at all. Quinn didn't even notice she was gone.

"Ow, Q." Julius was the first one to speak, lifting his head and shaking it from side to side. "No kneepads."

"Yeah, bud. Kneepads would have been good here."

It wasn't until Quinn got to her feet that she realized Nick had made it up onto the roof, and he was staring at her head. So was Tommy.

Julius wasn't staring at Quinn's head. He was staring into space, flapping his hands. But Nick and Tommy were definitely staring at her head.

"I have alopecia," Quinn said. Her whole body was trembling, but her voice was strangely calm as she bent down to rescue Guinevere. "It's an autoimmune disorder. Don't worry. It's not contagious."

. . . . . .

In the living room, after it was all over—after the four of them had descended from the roof, after Quinn had poured four glasses of orange juice—Julius curled up on the couch and fell asleep.

"He's out for the count," Tommy said.

"That happens sometimes," Quinn said, "when he's overstimulated."

Nick was standing in the doorway. He hadn't said much since they got downstairs. He hadn't said a word about Quinn's head. She'd considered putting Guinevere back on, but then she thought, what's the point? She wasn't getting any balder.

After a minute of them standing in silence, watching Julius sleep, Tommy said, "You were great up there."

"Me?" Quinn said.

"Yeah, you."

"So were you. If he'd jumped . . . if he'd fallen . . ." Quinn shivered. She didn't want to think about that. "You saved him."

Nick started applauding from the doorway, one of those slow-motion claps. "My brother the hero."

"I'm no hero," Tommy said.

"*Sure* you are, Tom," Nick said. "You prevented a horrible tragedy. *Imagine* what would have happened if you hadn't been there."

"Sarcasm noted," Tommy said. "Thanks."

"Oh, you think I'm being sarcastic? What makes you think that? Are you a mind reader?"

Tommy looked at Quinn. "I'm sorry," he said quietly.

Quinn shook her head. "It's okay."

"What are you apologizing for, Tom? You're not apologizing for *me*, are you?" Nick pressed a hand to his chest. "For *my* behavior?"

"Jesus, Nicky," Tommy muttered.

"Oh, now you're blaming *Jesus*? Nice, Tom. Real nice."

193

Quinn wasn't sure what to do. Should she ask them to take it outside? She glanced over at Julius. He was still asleep, three blankets pulled up to his chin, face soft, blond hair tufting out on the couch pillow. Sleeping, Julius looked like any other kid. Exactly like any other kid.

"You know something, Nick?" Tommy said. "I'm getting pretty sick of this crap."

"Oh yeah? What crap is that?"

Quinn watched the muscles in Tommy's jaw clench. "You know what crap."

"*This* crap?" Nick lifted one of his prosthetic legs in the air. "This crap right here? Is this the crap you're talking about?"

"Yeah. That's the crap I'm talking about."

"Right." Nick lowered his leg to the floor. "Well, I'm sorry that my amputated limbs are getting on your nerves."

Tommy took a deep breath and looked Nick straight in the eye. "It was an *accident*. I didn't *mean* to hurt you. I have apologized a thousand times over. What more do you want from me?"

"I want you to know what it's like! I want you to feel *pain*! That's what I want!"

"So hit me!"

Nick snorted. "Hit you?"

Tommy stepped forward. He raised both arms out to his sides. "Hit me. As hard as you can."

"Can I use an ax?"

"You guys," Quinn said. "Come on." But it was like they couldn't hear her, like she wasn't even there.

Nick took one step toward Tommy, then another. "Squat," he said.

"What?"

"Squat down. You're too tall."

Tommy widened his stance. He bent his knees like one of those Olympic weight lifters. "How's this?"

"Good."

"You guys," Quinn said again.

But Nick was already raising a fist in the air, letting it fly. He connected with Tommy's shoulder, just barely, stumbling a little on his metal feet.

"Come on," Tommy said, waggling his fingers toward himself. "You're a quarterback, Strout. You can do better than that."

"I'm not." Nick huffed through his nose. "A quarterback. Anymore."

"Stop," Quinn said. "This is crazy."

Nick regained his balance. He cocked his arm.

"Do it," Tommy said.

"*Stop*," Quinn said as Nick's fist sailed through the air again. This time he hit Tommy square in the face. Quinn heard a pop, like the sound of a carrot when you bite it in half. Tommy's head snapped back and his legs collapsed underneath him. Quinn watched in stunned silence as blood came gushing out of Tommy's nose and onto the hardwood.

From the floor, Tommy let out a few choice words before lifting his shirt to his face to catch the blood. "Well . . . ?"

"Well, what?" Nick said.

"Do you feel better?"

"Yeah." Nick nodded slowly. He looked a little dazed. "I do, actually."

"Good. 'Cause I'm pretty sure you broke my nose."

Quinn ran to the kitchen and grabbed a dish towel. She brought it back for Tommy. "Here. Keep the pressure on. That'll slow the bleeding."

He clutched the towel to his face and groaned.

"Should you . . ." Quinn hesitated. "Call your parents?"

Tommy shook his head, eyes squinting in pain. "I can drive to the hospital."

"Are you sure?"

He nodded, wincing again. "Yeah."

"I'd come with you if . . . you know . . ." Quinn glanced at Julius, asleep on the couch. There was no way she was waking him up.

" 'T's okay."

"Here," Nick said gruffly, reaching out his hand.

Tommy looked at him.

"Take it," Nick barked.

"Why, so you can drop me on my ass?"

"I won't do that."

Tommy took Nick's hand, and Nick yanked him up. The towel fell to the floor. Tommy's nose was crooked and still gushing blood.

"Jesus," Nick muttered. "Mom's gonna freak."

"Yeah." Tommy bent down to retrieve the towel and pressed it to his face again. "Dad'll be impressed, though."

"Are you sure you don't want to call them?" Quinn said. "Or an ambulance?"

"Nah," Nick said, throwing an arm around Tommy's waist. "We got this."

"Text me from the hospital?" Quinn said.

"Yeah," Nick said.

. . . . . .

Quinn had all the blood cleaned up by the time her dad got home. She was sitting in the chair next to Julius, rereading Nick's texts from the hospital—Septal fracture. No football for 3 wks. Sry abt the blood on ur floor.—when she heard footsteps behind her. "Hey, kiddo." A warm hand on her head. "How'd it go?"

"Shhh." Quinn gestured to the couch. "He's been asleep since six-fifteen."

"Really?" Quinn's dad glanced at his watch.

"What time is it?"

"Eight forty-two. Is he sick?"

"He's fine," Quinn said. "Long story, but he tried to set a Guinness World Record up on the roof."

"*What?*"

"Yeah. Highest BASE jump. It was pretty crazy . . . How was your dinner?"

"Whoa, whoa, whoa," Quinn's dad said. He gestured for Quinn to follow him into the kitchen. When they were seated at the table, he said, "The whole story, please. From the beginning."

Quinn didn't want to tell the whole story, but she knew that she had to. So she told it. The only part she left out was Nick cold-cocking Tommy and leaving a gallon of blood on the living room floor, because that had nothing to do with Julius.

"I'm sorry," Quinn said. "I screwed up."

Her dad shook his head. "No. *I'm* sorry. I never should have put you in that position."

"I shouldn't have let him out of my sight. I didn't know . . . I had no idea he would pull something like that."

"Neither did I."

"How does Mom do it?"

Her dad shook his head again. "I don't know."

"Are you going to tell her you left him with me? That he ended up on the roof?"

"Yes."

"She's going to freak."

"Maybe."

"Can't we just . . . keep it between us?"

"Q," her dad said. "I can't do that."

"Why not?"

"Because your mom and I are a team. You know that, right? We're in this parenting thing together."

Quinn was just starting to roll her eyes when Julius appeared in the doorway to the kitchen, blinking in the light.

"Phil," Julius said. His voice sounded croaky. "Where's Mo?"

"Mo's in Arizona. Remember, bud? She went on an airplane."

Quinn could tell just from looking at her dad that he wanted to throw his arms around her brother and hold him for a good ten minutes. But this was Julius. Julius didn't do hugs.

"I want Mo, Phil."

"So do I," Quinn's dad said.

. . . . .

Later, Quinn's dad knocked on her door.

"Q? You still up?"

"Yeah," Quinn said. It was almost eleven o'clock, but she couldn't sleep.

"Can I come in?"

"Yeah." She clicked on her bedside light.

Her dad opened the door. He was back to wearing his Bon Jovi concert T-shirt and a pair of holey sweats. "Hi."

Quinn waved from the bed. "Is Jules asleep?"

"Not yet. He's in bed, reading."

"What if he goes up on the roof again?"

"I don't think he'll do that. It's dark out."

Quinn nodded. He was right. Julius wasn't a fan of the dark.

Her dad perched on the end of her bed. He didn't say anything at first, just sat there, clearing his throat.

Quinn waited. This was definitely weird.

"So, I read your post on the . . . ah . . . Alopecia Sucks website."

"What?" Quinn sat up.

"I wasn't snooping," her dad said quickly. "I just turned on my computer, and there it was."

Quinn shook her head. Was that possible? Had she not logged out?

"Q." Her dad squeezed her foot through the blanket. "Why didn't you tell us what was going on with you in Boulder?"

Quinn shrugged. "Because you couldn't have fixed it."

"But your mom and I had no idea. How could we not have known any of this was happening? If you'd told us, we could have . . ." He hesitated.

"What, Dad? What could you have done?"

"Called the school. Talked to some parents."

Quinn rolled her eyes. "Really, Dad? You would have called up Ethan Hess's parents and said, 'Tell your son to stop telling

200

the world that my daughter gives new meaning to the word *head*'?"

Her dad cringed. "No one has the right to spread rumors about you, Quinn. And no one has the right to touch you. Not without your permission."

"I know that," Quinn said.

"Do you?"

"It wasn't a big deal." She thought about Ethan's hand, reaching out to grab her boob through her shirt. It had felt like nothing. He might as well have grabbed her elbow.

"I disagree," her dad said.

"He didn't force me to do anything."

"It doesn't matter if he forced you. He touched your body without your consent. And he tried to get you to touch him. That's not okay. That's—"

"Dad," Quinn said. "I *know.* They covered this in health class."

"They did?"

"Good touch, bad touch. No means no." Quinn's father was so clueless, she almost felt bad for him. "I didn't tell you about that night because I didn't want you to know. Because the whole thing was stupid. I thought that when we moved here . . ." Quinn's voice trailed off.

"What?" her dad said.

"Nothing. It's dumb."

"I bet it's not."

"I thought I could start over. I thought if I wore the wig, no one would ever have to know, and now . . ."

Her dad's eyebrows lifted.

"It fell off, when we were up on the roof. People saw."

"Which people?"

"Nick and Tommy."

"So . . . two people?"

"Three, if you count Julius."

"Quinn."

"What?"

"Sweetheart. Do you really think Nick and Tommy are going to shun you now? Do you think they're going to run off to school and tell everyone you wear a wig?"

Quinn thought about this. She thought of Nick running off to school, literally, on his short prosthetic legs with training feet. She thought about Nick and Tommy in her living room, squatting, throwing punches, acting out their own family drama.

"No," she said. "I don't think they will."

CHAPTER
18

WHEN QUINN CAME DOWN FOR BREAKFAST, the first thing she saw was the clock over the sink. "*Nine-oh-five?*" she said. "Why didn't you wake me?"

"You needed to sleep," her dad said. He was standing at the stove, holding a spatula.

"School started an hour ago!" Quinn looked around the kitchen for her backpack. Usually she hung it on a hook by the door, but it wasn't there. "Where's my backpack?"

"Take a load off," her dad said. "You're not going to school."

"Why not?"

"Mental health day."

"For me or for you?"

"For all of us."

Julius shuffled into the kitchen, hair sticking up, headphones dangling from his neck. "It's fried Friday, Phil."

"Yes, it is, my friend," Quinn's dad said. He gestured to the stovetop. "Fried eggs, over easy. Fried hash browns."

Julius shuffled over to the table. He pulled out a chair. "With Heinz tomato ketchup?"

"What good are fried hash browns without Heinz tomato ketchup?"

"They are not much good, Phil."

Quinn's dad set a plate down on the table. Julius clamped his headphones to his ears and picked up the ketchup.

Quinn looked at her dad. "You're following Mom's instructions now?"

"I am."

"What happened to Phil's rules?"

"I'm choosing my battles."

Quinn looked at her brother, squeezing half the bottle of ketchup onto his plate. "What are we supposed to do all day?" she said.

"Well," her dad said, "in about three hours we're going to go pick up your mom at the airport."

"We are?"

"We are."

Quinn nodded slowly. "You told her about the roof."

"I did."

"Did she freak?"

"She was concerned, yes."

"Is that why she's coming home today?"

"In part. But also because your uncle Andrew is flying in tonight."

"From Australia?"

"Yes. He'll be staying with Gigi for a few weeks."

"Huh," Quinn said.

"How about some eggs?"

"Okay."

"Hash browns?"

"Sure." Quinn walked over to the fridge to get herself some juice. That was when she noticed something on the wall. "Hey. You put up the whiteboard."

"I did."

Quinn read the words aloud. *"Felix culpa."* She looked at her dad, who was transferring eggs onto a plate.

"Happy fault. An apparent disaster that ends up having surprisingly positive consequences. I thought it was apropos."

"Why?"

"We're working on goal-setting with Julius," her dad said, putting the plate on the table. "Granted, BASE jumping off a three-story house with no safety equipment is an incredibly dangerous, poorly thought-out goal. But your brother deciding, on his own, to set a world record? That's . . ."

"Crazy?" Quinn offered.

"I was going to say *remarkable*. Setting a world record is a remarkable goal, for anyone. But especially for Julius."

Quinn pulled out a chair and sat down.

"We just need to help him choose something a little less . . ."

"Crazy?"

"I was going to say *hazardous.*"

Quinn took a bite of eggs, chewed, swallowed. "The world's biggest pile of marshmallows?"

"Something like that."

. . . . .

From the curbside pickup lane, which they'd already driven through three times because the airport police kept telling them to move, Quinn finally spotted her mom's denim jacket and red wheelie suitcase.

"Mom!" Quinn stuck her head out the window—her bald, cue-ball head, wearing nothing but her ratty Colorado Rockies baseball cap. "Mo!"

"Mom. Mo," Julius repeated, even though he wasn't looking anywhere but down at his book. "Mom. Mo."

"Did you miss us?" Quinn asked as soon as her mom had put her suitcase in the trunk and slid into the front passenger seat. "I feel like you've been gone forever."

"Me, too," Quinn's dad said, leaning over the gearshift for a kiss.

"Me three," Julius said.

They all turned to look at him.

"Did he just say 'me three'?" Quinn's dad asked, ignoring the airport police officer blowing his whistle.

"Me four. Me five. Me six." Julius tapped out a little beat on top of *Guinness World Records 2017*. "Mom Mo Mom Mo Mom Mo."

"Mom," Quinn said. "He's saying he missed you."

"Buddy." Mo turned in her seat to look at Julius. "I'm—"

"MOVE OUT!" The officer was now banging on the hood of the Subaru. "MOVE OUT NOW!"

"Sheesh," Quinn's dad muttered, nosing the car forward. "We're having a moment here."

"Bud," Mo tried again. "Julius . . . Could I have some eye contact, please?"

Julius lifted his head and looked, from Quinn's vantage point anyway, at Mo's ear. Ear contact.

"I missed you so much," her mom said. "I missed you to the moon and back."

"The youngest moon rocks date back some three point two billion years. They are a type of volcanic basalt, originating from the dark lunar seas. They are not dissimilar to the age of the oldest datable rocks on Earth."

Mo nodded, smiling. "That's a very cool fact."

"It's not cool, Mo. It's hot. Very, very hot. It takes higher than two thousand two hundred degrees Fahrenheit to make moon rocks."

"Like a kiln," Mo said.

"Like a kiln," Julius said. Then his head snapped back down and the headphones went on.

. . . . .

When they got home, Quinn's mom asked Quinn to come upstairs with her. "Keep me company while I unpack," she said. But Quinn knew what this really meant. It had nothing to do with unpacking.

"I'm sorry," Quinn said as soon as she walked into her parents' room, before her mom could say anything. "The roof was my fault. It was my job to watch him, and I let him out of my sight. I know it was bad. Trust me, nothing you say right now could make me feel any worse than I already do."

"We'll talk about that in a minute," her mom said.

"What?"

"I want to talk about something else first." Quinn's mom sat down on the bed. She patted the space beside her. "It's important."

"Okay . . . ," Quinn said. She didn't like the sound of this, something more important than her brother's safety and well-being. She sat down next to her mom. "What is it?"

Mo was wearing her serious face. "Did he hurt you? The boy?" For a second, Quinn assumed that the "boy" she was referring to was Nick. Maybe some of the blood from Nick punching Tommy was still on the living room floor, and her mom saw it and thought the blood was Quinn's. But then her mom said, "From the Valentine's party."

"*Ethan Hess?* Oh my God, Dad told you about that?" Quinn flopped back on the bed. "The stupid message board?"

"I don't think it's stupid," her mom said.

"Yes, it is. I told Dad, the whole thing was ridiculous. I just want to forget it ever happened."

"Did Ethan hurt you?"

"No, he didn't *hurt* me. God." Quinn groaned and pressed a pillow to her face, which made her words come out muffled. "And if he'd tried to, I would have squeezed his nuts until they shriveled up like raisins."

Quinn's mom let out a hoot. "Excuse me?"

"I read this article once." Quinn flung the pillow off her face and spoke to the ceiling. "If a guy tries to attack you, you're supposed to grab his testicles with all five of your fingers and squeeze as hard as you can. You should really dig in, too, with your nails." She sat up to demonstrate. "Then you *twist* and *pull*. It's supposed to be extremely painful."

"Yes. I'm sure." Quinn's mom shook her head, smiling a little. "I had no idea you knew that."

"There's a lot you don't know about me."

"Honey . . . why didn't you tell me what was going on in Boulder? Why didn't you talk to me?"

"Because," Quinn said slowly. "I *told* you. It was stupid. And you're always . . . you know . . ."

"What?"

Quinn sat there on the bed and thought of a million different ways she could say it. Her mom was just looking at her, eyebrows raised like she had no clue.

Finally, Quinn said, "You're always busy with Julius. And I know his problems are bigger than mine. I *know* they are. So I never want to bother you with stuff. I just try to figure it out on my own."

"Quinn."

"Yeah."

"Look at me."

"I am."

"I'm your mom."

"I know."

"I love you as much as I love your brother. Your problems are no less important to me than his are. Do you hear me?"

"Yes."

"You are *just as important to me*. I love you *just as much*. You can talk to me *anytime*. About *anything*. I will *always* make time for you."

Quinn willed her eyes not to roll. "Okay."

"Do you hear me?"

"Yes."

"Is there anything else you want to tell me about you?"

"No."

"Okay," her mom said. She nodded a few times. "Now I need to ask you about Julius."

"Do you have to?"

"I do. Yes. I don't blame you for what happened, Quinn. Believe me. Julius could have gotten up on the roof even if Dad and I had been home. But since you were the one who was here, I need you to step me through exactly what happened so I understand. I need to know what to tell his teachers. Okay?"

Quinn let out a breath. "Okay."

. . . . .

When Quinn and her mom came back downstairs, Julius was sitting at the kitchen table and Quinn's dad was unloading the dishwasher. "I've been thinking," he said, hanging one of Mo's ceramic coffee mugs on a hook. "We should thank Nick and Tommy for their help yesterday."

"I already thanked them," Quinn said.

"I didn't. Neither did your mom."

"Well, I did. So . . . they've been thanked."

"I'd like us to do it together," Quinn's dad persisted. "As a family. I'd like us to drive over there."

"To their *house*?"

"Yes."

"You want us to just *show up on their doorstep*?"

"We could call first."

Quinn stared at her dad. This didn't sound like him at all.

"I agree," Quinn's mom said. "I'd like to thank Nick and Tommy, too. And I'd like Julius to thank them."

Quinn glanced over at Julius, clamped into his headphones, mumbling at his book and paying no attention whatsoever to this conversation.

"Do you have the Strouts' phone number?" Mo said.

Quinn shook her head. There was no getting out of this. That much was clear. "I'll text Nick and find out if they're home."

"Sounds good," her dad said.

Quinn went up to her room to get her phone. She'd had it powered down since she went to bed last night. When she powered up, there were four new texts, all from Nick.

We're home. Mom flipping out abt T's nose. Dad thinks I was justified but says if I hit him agn I'm grounded for life.

How is Julius?

Hello? U there?

U mad?

Quinn texted back, He's ok. I'm not mad. R u and T home now? My parents want to come say thank u for ur help ystrdy.

Her phone pinged right away.

Nick: We're here.

Quinn: K. C u soon.

She checked herself in the mirror. Navy-blue shorts (fine). Yellow shirt with white stripes (fine). Rockies cap. Was she really going to do this? Was she actually going to walk onto Nick and Tommy's front porch wearing this ratty hat with nothing underneath?

Quinn looked at Guinevere, sitting in a lump on top of

212

her dresser. A few hairs had gotten ripped out by a roof shingle. Quinn picked up her wig comb and tried to smooth Guinevere out the way she'd been taught at Belle's Wig Botik. *Don't touch the wig cap. Brush from the ends before moving to the roots.* A clump of hair came out in Quinn's hand.

She froze. "Mom!" she yelled. "Mom!"

A few seconds later, Mo came running into the room. "Are you okay? What's wrong?"

Quinn held out the clump of hair. It felt like that first time, when her real hair started falling out.

"Honey, it's fine," her mom said. "We'll get it fixed. I still have the warranty."

Quinn shook her head. "What am I supposed to wear now?"

"What about your hat?"

Quinn shook her head again.

"Well." Mo picked up the other Styrofoam head that was sitting on the dresser. "What about this?"

213

CHAPTER
19

IT WAS OBVIOUSLY PRETTY WEIRD TO SPEND your first six weeks in a new town as a redhead and then suddenly show up as something else. But that's what Quinn was doing, showing up on the Strouts' front porch with a head of shiny black hair.

"Whoa," Nick said when he opened the door, even though Quinn had texted to tell him to prepare himself.

"Her name is Sasha." Quinn reached up to check that Sasha was still straight. "My old one was Guinevere. She got torn up on the roof. It was either this or a hat."

"Right."

In addition to his legs, Nick was wearing a hat. A blue knitted beanie. Maybe Quinn should have worn a blue knitted beanie. What was she thinking wearing a shiny black wig that made her look like Edna Mode from *The Incredibles*? That was what Julius had said the minute she came downstairs. "Edna Mode. 'No capes! No capes!'" Then he'd launched into the Guinness World Record for the longest cape.

"Do you think I look like Edna Mode from *The Incredibles*?"

Nick squinted at Quinn. "I think you look badass."

"You do?"

He made his voice deep. "Basketball player by day. Russian spy by night."

Quinn smiled. She knew he was just trying to make her feel better.

"Do your parents need help?" Nick looked past Quinn at the driveway. Her mom and dad were trying to coax Julius out of the car without touching him.

"They've got it," Quinn said.

It took a few minutes, but finally all four McAvoys were up on the Strouts' porch, and Quinn's mom was squeezing Nick's forearm. "Thank you, Nick . . . so much . . . for being there for Quinn and Julius yesterday."

"We can't thank you enough," Quinn's dad said.

Nick looked embarrassed. "I really didn't do anything. I just answered the phone when Quinn called. It was my brother who—"

"Hi." Tommy walked through the door and stood next to Nick. "I'm Tom. I don't usually look like this."

Quinn wondered if she should have warned her parents about Tommy's nose, but the truth was she hadn't expected him to look this bad. His nose was huge and swollen, like a potato stuck to the middle of his face. His eyes were puffy and bruised.

Quinn's mom sucked in a breath. "Julius didn't—did he *punch* you?"

Tommy smiled and shook his head. "No."

The air on the porch stood still. Quinn waited for Tommy to throw Nick under the bus. He didn't. She waited for Nick to take credit for Tommy's face. He didn't.

Quinn took it upon herself to break the silence. "Tommy," she said, "these are my parents, Maureen and Phil. Mom, Dad, this is Tommy."

"Phil McAvoy," Quinn's dad said, pumping Tommy's hand up and down. "We can't thank you enough for what you did yesterday."

"I didn't do that much. You should have seen Quinn up on the roof. The way she talked to her brother . . . the way she got him to listen . . . it was something."

"Yeah, okay," Quinn said. She was starting to feel embarrassed—even more embarrassed than she would normally feel, standing on someone's porch with her family, dressed like Edna Mode.

"Julius," Quinn's mom said. She turned to Quinn's brother, who was standing over by the porch swing, rocking from side to side. "Could you please thank Nick and Tommy and Q for their help yesterday? For getting you down from the roof so you didn't fall and hurt yourself?"

"Thank you for your help yesterday," Julius said to the porch swing.

"Could you please turn around and look them in the eye when you say it?"

"They have six eyes, Mo. I have two."

"Yes, well, you can look at Nick first, and then Tommy, and then Q."

Julius did one of his spin moves. "Thank you. Thank you. Thank you."

"They didn't want you to get hurt, bud," Quinn's mom continued. "That was a dangerous place for you to be, up on the roof. It's a long way down. The ground is hard."

This was what you had to do for Julius. You had to spell it out for him. And then you had to spell it out for everyone else, so they would understand why you were spelling it out for Julius.

"Julius doesn't sense danger the same way you and I do," Quinn's mom explained to Nick and Tommy. "His brain doesn't always identify and remember dangerous things. So we have to keep reminding him of what those things are."

Nick and Tommy nodded. Julius rocked and snapped. Quinn resisted the urge to list all the dangerous things Julius wasn't afraid of but should be. Speeding cars. Knives. Hot stoves. He still had scars on his hand from the time he climbed up on the counter and pressed his palm to the burner. Quinn hated thinking about that.

"Anyway," Quinn's mom said. "We just wanted to thank you both in person, for helping to keep Julius safe."

"You're welcome," Tommy and Nick said, basically in unison.

"You're welcome," Julius said to the side of the house.

Quinn looked at Julius, his skinny white neck, his tufty blond hair, and felt suddenly, unbearably sad. She wanted to shake her brother until he understood. *You can't jump off a roof! Don't you get it?! You could have cracked your skull! You could have broken your neck!* She wanted to shake him the way you shook an Etch A Sketch, until the screen was clear. But you couldn't do that with Julius. You couldn't reset his screen.

Quinn looked at her brother and, with all her powers of telepathy, she told him, *I love you.* Then, *Stay off the effing roof.*

"Well," Quinn's dad said. "We should probably get going."

"Hey." Nick was looking at Quinn. He must have seen something in her face, the tears pressing on the backs of her eyeballs, threatening to fall. "You can stay if you want."

"Yeah?"

Nick gave her a quick smile, the kind you give someone when her parents are watching. "My mom can drop you off later," he said, "when she gets back from her errands."

Quinn looked at Mo. "Is that okay?"

Mo nodded.

218

Quinn said, "I know you just got home, but—"

"Stay," Mo said. "Have fun."

"Okay. I will."

. . . . .

Quinn followed Nick up the stairs. It was slow going, but not as slow as it had been the last time she saw him go up steps.

"You've been practicing," Quinn said.

"Yeah," Nick said.

His room was the first doorway on the right. Big bed with a brown-and-white comforter that looked like a giant football. Desk with a football-shaped lamp. Dresser with miniature football drawer pulls. And about a hundred football players tacked up on the walls.

"I'm sensing a theme here," Quinn said as she walked in.

"Ha-ha."

Quinn walked over to a coatrack made to look like a goalpost. Four of Nick's sweatshirts were hanging from the hooks. "This is cool."

"I hate it."

"This?" Quinn ran her fingers along the coatrack.

"All of it."

Quinn looked at Nick. His cheeks were pink. "My parents want me to move back up here, but I just . . . all this crap . . ." He waved his hands through the air. "I can't stand looking at it."

Quinn crossed the room and stood in front of some sweaty football player with eye black running down his face and the word *unstoppable* printed across his forehead. She pulled four thumbtacks out of the wall and rolled him up into a tube. She handed the tube to Nick. "How's that?"

Nick shook his head. He unrolled the tube and ripped the sweaty football player in half.

"Yeah?" Quinn said.

He nodded.

They started tearing posters off the walls. Nick did the low ones. Quinn did the high ones. They tore and ripped until there was nothing left but blue paint and a million tack holes.

"Better?" Quinn said. She was hot from all the tearing. She could feel her scalp, damp and prickly under her wig. She hated that feeling. But it was worth it to see the look on Nick's face.

"Better," he said, grinning. He took a few hobbles through the mess of torn-up paper and over to the bed, where he yanked off the football comforter and dropped it onto the floor in a big lump.

Quinn looked at the white sheets. "Tabula rasa," she said.

"What?"

"Clean slate."

"Yeah." Nick scooted back on the bed, his legs sticking straight out in front of him.

Quinn lowered herself to the floor, on top of the football comforter.

They were both quiet for a minute. Then he said, "Why didn't you tell me?"

Quinn knew without having to ask. She shook her head, feeling Sasha brush against her cheeks. "I'm not sure."

"I don't care, you know."

Quinn looked at him.

"You don't have to wear that thing if you don't want. Not in front of me."

Quinn's hand went reflexively to her head.

"I mean, not that it looks *bad*. It doesn't. The other one didn't, either. Just . . . you don't have to be embarrassed."

Quinn nodded slowly. "Okay."

"Does it itch?"

Quinn raised her eyebrows.

"I did some googling."

"Sometimes," she said. "Yeah." Then, "Do your legs hurt? I mean, where they used to be?"

Nick looked surprised.

"I did some googling, too."

"Sometimes," he said. "Especially at night."

"That sucks."

Nick shrugged. "I'm used to it . . . My hand hurts more, actually."

"Your hand?"

"From punching Tommy."

"Right." Quinn nodded. "I'll bet his nose hurts more than your hand."

221

"His nose is nothing."

"It doesn't look like nothing."

"He'll be fine in three weeks."

Quinn looked at Nick. He looked at her. The blue walls all around them made it feel like they were underwater.

After a minute, Quinn said, "I want to tell you something. As your friend."

"Okay."

"You might not want to hear this, but I'm going to say it anyway . . . I think you need to let it go."

"What?"

"Tommy. You need to forgive him."

Nick frowned. "Easy for you to say."

"Actually, it's *not*. I've been thinking it for a while. I just didn't think it was any of my business."

Quinn waited for Nick to say that she was right; it wasn't her business. But he stayed quiet. So she kept going. "I know I wasn't there that night. And I can't imagine what it was like for you. But . . . it was an accident, just a horrible accident."

"He was drinking."

"I know."

"What you don't know is that I *knew* he was drunk. I knew, and I got on anyway."

Quinn looked at Nick's very serious face and said, "It's not your fault." She pictured him hopping on the back of the snowmobile. She pictured herself, Snapchatting away while

222

Julius climbed up onto the roof. "Sometimes bad stuff just happens."

Nick made a sound. Not a snort, exactly, more like air leaking out of a balloon. *Phhhhhht.* He flopped back on the bed.

Quinn waited.

Nothing.

"Tommy's a good guy," she continued. "He just did a stupid thing. And from what I can tell . . . he's trying really hard to make it up to you."

Silence.

Quinn stopped talking. Maybe she'd said too much. Should she have just kept her mouth shut? It was none of her business. It really wasn't.

Nick sat up suddenly. "Are you hot for Tommy?"

"What?"

"You heard me," Nick said. Then, "Forget it. I don't want to know."

Quinn hesitated. She really thought about it. "No," she said finally. "I am not hot for Tommy."

"You're not?"

"No."

"Good," Nick said.

They were quiet again. After a minute, Quinn said, "What made you think I was?"

"I don't know. All the girls are."

"In case you haven't noticed," Quinn said, "I'm not like all the girls."

CHAPTER
20

WHAT WAS SHE GOING TO SAY TO EVERYONE? What, oh, what was she going to say? Quinn had spent the past seventy-two hours fielding texts from Ivy and Carmen and Lissa. Whr r u? Y wrnt u in school? U ok? R u sick? When she'd texted back that she was taking a few mental health days, she received a flurry of heart and flower and smiley emojis, and a bunch of we miss u and get btr soon texts, which obviously made her feel good. But also kind of crappy. Just like on the first day of school, when she'd debated and debated in front of the mirror about what to wear on her head, she did the same thing this morning. Except now she actually had friends. Now she had something to lose.

Walking down the freshman hall, Quinn took a deep breath. Sasha might not look like her natural hair, but she was better than a hat. By far. A hat was just a Band-Aid, waiting to get ripped off.

Ivy and Carmen and Lissa were standing at Quinn's locker.

"Hey," Carmen said, when Quinn stepped in to spin her lock. 38-17-5. "What are you doing?"

"Hi," Quinn said, jerking open the door.

"That's not your lockah."

"Uh, yeah, it is," Quinn said.

"Oh my gawd." Ivy clapped a hand to her mouth. "I totally didn't recognize you."

"Is it my new lip gloss?" Quinn deadpanned.

"You changed your hair," Lissa said. "Like, completely."

"Yeah." Quinn reached up, tucked Sasha behind one ear. "It was time for a change."

"You look . . ." Ivy hesitated.

"Like Edna Mode from *The Incredibles*?"

"No. Did you evah see that show *Alias*?"

Quinn shook her head. Sasha brushed against her cheeks.

"Is that the one with those freaky space dudes?" Lissa said.

"*Alias*," Carmen said. "Not *Aliens*."

"My mom's been binge-watching it on Hulu," Ivy said. "She's obsessed. It's about this . . . whaddaya call it . . ."

"Alien?" Lissa said.

Carmen snorted.

"No"—Ivy snapped her fingers—"*double agent*. Who works for the CIA and is always changing her hair so she can

225

carry out her secret missions." Ivy turned to Quinn. "You made me think of her because she's really tall and pretty and one of her hairdos looks just like that. What's her name? . . . starts with an *S* . . ." Ivy snapped her fingers again. "*Sydney Bristow*. Nailed it."

"Huh," Quinn said. That was all she could get out. *Huh.*

. . . . . .

At lunch, Lissa asked the question Quinn had been waiting for. "It's a wig, right?" she said, dipping french fries in ketchup and shoving them into her mouth.

Quinn was midbite. She finished chewing her apple and set it down. "Yeah," she said. Because what was she going to do, lie? "It's a wig."

"Thank gawd," Carmen said, clutching her hand to her chest like a really bad actress. "If you'd told me that you'd dyed that beautiful red hair black . . . that would be a tragedy."

Quinn picked up her apple again.

"So, wait," Ivy said. "There is no way you stuffed all your hair under there. Did you cut it?"

"Oh my gawd," Lissa said. "Did you get a really bad haircut? That happened to me once when I asked for bangs. It looked so bad. Remembah, you guys? Sixth grade? I cried for like a week."

"You did look pretty bad," Ivy said. "No offense."

"None taken," Lissa said. "A wig is actually a *really* good idea for bad hair days. I wish I'd thought of that when I got bangs . . ."

"Where'd you buy it, Quinn?" Carmen asked, going in for some of Lissa's fries. "Amazon?"

"Um. Back in Colorado."

"What did it run ya?" Ivy said. "Twenty bucks? Thirty?"

"A little more than that," Quinn murmured.

"Well," Carmen said, "I have to say you're pulling it off. Not many natural redheads would look good with black hair, but your skin has a little olive to it, which is very uncommon for redheads."

"I'm not a redhead," Quinn said.

"Fine. Strawberry blond, whatevah."

Quinn stared at her apple, swallowed hard. "I used to be sort of dirty blond. A little lighter in the summers. But not red at all, really."

"So you color it?"

Quinn shook her head, trying to find the courage to look up from her apple. If she didn't say it now, she'd still have to say it sometime. Maybe in a month. Maybe in a year. She was just delaying the inevitable. "It all fell out. Last summer."

Quinn felt a hand on her arm. She looked up.

"What do you mean, it all fell out?" Ivy said.

"I mean . . ." Quinn locked eyes with Ivy's sparkly hoop earring. "I have an autoimmune disorder. It's called alopecia areata. You can't catch it from me. It doesn't hurt or anything. It just makes my hair fall out."

No one said anything for what felt like an eternity. Then Carmen blurted, "Lissa was born with eleven toes."

"Carm!" Lissa whacked Carmen in the shoulder.

"What? It's true! You came out with a freaky extra toe and the doctah chopped it off and now your feet look semi-normal."

"Thanks a lot," Lissa huffed. "I told you that in confidence."

"Sorry." Carmen shrugged and reached for a french fry. "It just slipped out."

"You think you can eat my fries now?"

"We're best friends. We share everything."

"Not anymore we don't."

Everyone at the table was laughing, even Lissa. Carmen winked at Quinn. For some reason, she felt tears spring into her eyes.

"Hey." Ivy was nudging her arm again. "You okay?"

Quinn nodded. She'd actually done it. She'd told them. And nothing bad had happened. There had been no sideways glances, no lame excuses to get up from the table and whisper about her in a corner. Maybe that would still happen, but so far everyone was acting normal. Well, not *normal*. These girls were weird, no question. For one thing, they never stopped talking. And they were constantly putting on lip gloss.

"You want?" Carmen said, holding out her little wand to Quinn. "This is a great color for you if you're planning to stay a brunette. It's called Potent Plum."

"Thanks," Quinn said, slicking some on.

"My favorite aunt wears a wig," Carmen said.

"She does?"

"Yup. Has for years."

"Is she sick?" Quinn said.

"Nope. She just doesn't like her hair."

"Really?"

"Really," Carmen said. "Her wig's pretty cool, too. It's sort of coppery brown. It brings out her earth tones."

There were moments when people surprised you. Today was full of those moments.

CHAPTER
21

THE THIRD WEEK OF OCTOBER, QUINN received two notices in homeroom. One was for winter sports tryouts. The other was for the art show.

"Did you see this?" Carmen said in PE, waving the tryouts permission form in Quinn's face. "You're going out for hoops, right?"

"Yes," Quinn said.

"Good," Carmen said.

"Me and Liss will cheer you guys on," Ivy said. "Won't we, Liss?"

"Of course." Lissa reached out to pat Sasha, but gently. Quinn had told them about the wig tape. They knew everything now. They knew, and they didn't care.

. . . . .

"Did you see this?" Quinn said in study hall, sliding the art show announcement onto Nick's desk. "November fifth. They want submissions."

"So?"

"So, you should submit one of your drawings."

Nick shook his head. "I don't do shows."

"What do you mean, you 'don't do shows'? From what I hear, you used to put on a show every Friday night on the football field."

"That was different."

"You don't want to share your art with the world?"

"No. I don't."

Quinn knew Nick well enough now to read his cues. He wanted her to shut up about the art show, just like he wanted her to shut up about him wearing his legs to school. So Quinn shut up. She would text him about it later. Nick was better at texting than talking anyway. It had become a tradition. Every night, when they were lying in their separate beds, they texted each other. Sometimes about little stuff, like math home-work, sometimes about big stuff. In the dark, under the covers, that was when it got interesting.

Like the time Nick texted Quinn about this dream he kept having, where he was at football practice and he was running. How he could hear his coach blowing his whistle. He could feel the huff of his own breath, the spit forming in the cor-ners of his mouth, the cramp in his legs. He was running so fast, faster than he'd ever run, faster than anyone. And then he woke up. He looked under the blanket. The ache was still there, but his legs weren't. And he wanted them back so bad, it was like a bomb exploded inside him. He wanted to slam his fists into the wall until his knuckles popped, until he saw blood. Because the pain in his legs wasn't real and he needed to feel something that was.

Or the time Quinn texted Nick about the names she was called back in Boulder. About John Kugler ripping the hat off her head in assembly. About everyone laughing.

Twice, Nick texted Quinn pictures of his room. He had a new comforter now, blue with red stripes. He'd tacked some of his art on the walls. Not the leg drawings, but other things. The tree in his backyard. A bird, spreading its wings in flight.

I like ur bird, Quinn texted.

Thx, Nick texted back. Me too.

. . . . .

"Can you sign this?" Quinn asked her mom after school. Mo was in the studio, her hands deep in the clay.

"Bring it closer," she said.

Quinn held the permission form in front of her mom's face.

"You want to try out for the basketball team?"

"Yeah."

"That's great, Q. That's really great." Mo was giving her

this look. She'd been doing it a lot lately, gazing at Quinn with shiny eyes.

"What's with the look?" Quinn said.

"What look? There's no look."

"There's a look. You're doing it right now. You're *gazing* at me."

"What—a mother can't gaze at her own daughter?" Mo reached out her clay-covered fingers like she was going to grab Quinn. "Come here and give me a hug."

Quinn jumped back. "No touching!" Then she laughed. "I sound like Julius."

"Do you know where Julius is right now?" her mom said, going back to her clay head.

"Is this a test?"

"Julius is on a playdate."

Quinn looked at her mom. "Did you just say 'Julius is on a playdate'?"

Mo smiled. "Her name is Randa. She goes to the Cove."

"Randa?"

"Short for Miranda, I imagine. Her mother is lovely. We met last week for coffee."

"Huh," Quinn said. Julius was on a playdate. She couldn't remember him ever getting invited to someone else's house. "What are they going to do?"

"I don't know," Mo said. "Eat snacks. Play games. Whatever kids do on playdates."

"Julius doesn't *play games*. And what about the food? Does Randa's mother know what he eats?"

"I made her a list. She's used to this, honey. Randa has many of the same challenges."

Quinn shook her head. "If you say so."

"Would you scratch my back? I have an itch, right in the middle, and I don't want to get clay on my shirt."

"Sure," Quinn said. "If I can get new basketball sneakers for tryouts."

"What's wrong with your old ones?"

"I just want to start fresh, you know? I want good juju."

"Good juju." Quinn's mom was wiggling on her stool. "I understand. Now scratch. Please."

"Is that a yes?"

"That's a yes. Yes."

Quinn scratched Mo's back, hard through her flannel shirt.

"Up a little . . . to the left . . . a little more . . . ahhh."

"Better?" Quinn said.

"Much. Thanks."

" 'Kay, well. I'm gonna go get a snack."

"There's a package waiting for you on the kitchen table."

"For me?"

Mo smiled. "I think you'll be happy."

. . . . .

The package was a cardboard box. The return address was *Belle's Wig Botik, Denver, CO*. And inside, on top of a pile of packing peanuts, was a sheet of white paper. It read:

Dear Quinn,
We have successfully mended your Estetica human hair
wig. We hope that you will be pleased with our work.
Please remember to follow the DOs and DON'Ts of
proper human hair wig care to ensure that your Estetica
wig lives a long and happy life.
DO: Use ceramic-plated heat tools to curl and straighten
your hair.
DO NOT: Try to perm or relax the hair. Chemical
processing could ruin the wig.
DO: Wash your wig every 8–14 days, or as needed.
Using a dry shampoo can help you go longer between
washings when sprayed on the interior of the cap. We do
not recommend spraying dry shampoo on the outside of
human hair wigs.

Quinn stopped reading. The list went on and on. It was making her tired just looking at it. Taking Guinevere out of the packing peanuts made her feel tired, too. Guinevere was heavier than Sasha, which meant more wig tape. More wig tape meant more itch. More itch meant more trips to the bathroom to witch-hazel her head. The truth was that Quinn didn't want to deal with any of it. Not Guinevere. Not Sasha. Not the washing every eight to fourteen days. Not the gently wrapping her damp wig in a towel and patting it to remove excess water. None of it. Quinn wanted to be free, like the bird on Nick's wall. She wanted to zoom down the street on her skateboard without worrying that her wig would fly off. She wanted to soar through the air toward the basketball hoop without worrying about some girl's bracelet getting stuck in her wig hair.

What would happen? This was the drumbeat running through Quinn's mind. What would happen if she showed up at school with nothing on her head? No Guinevere. No Sasha. No hat. Nothing. She knew Nick would be fine with it. He'd seen her head already. She was 90 percent sure Ivy and Carmen and Lissa would be cool—weirded out, maybe, at first. They would be funny about it, though. Carmen would suggest a new lip gloss. But what about everyone else? What about the kids Quinn knew by name but didn't really know? What about the three Emmas, and the two Avas, and Kacey, and Kylie, and Kelsie, and Chelsey? What about Jack, and Zach, and Mason, and Carson, and Tyler, and Darius? What about Griff, Nick's old friend from the football team? All it took was one mean kid. All it took was one nickname.

No one had said much when Quinn showed up wearing Sasha. Emma from homeroom had asked if Quinn was celebrating Halloween early, but she hadn't said it in a sarcastic way, more like she was curious. A boy in Quinn's social studies class had told Quinn that she looked like Katy Perry, and Quinn was 87 percent sure this was a compliment. Emma from art class had said, "I like how you keep changing your look." By Quinn's calculations, she had only changed her look once, from Guinevere to Sasha, but then Emma went on to explain, "Sometimes you're sporty. Sometimes you're super-modely. You just do your own thing. It's cool."

Would art-class Emma think it was cool if Quinn showed up bald? Quinn had no clue. Showing up to school bald when you had no clue how people were going to react was like skateboarding down the street blindfolded and hoping you won't get hit. Quinn wasn't that stupid.

CHAPTER
22

IT WAS FUNNY HOW THE GYM AT GULLS Head High School smelled exactly like the gym at Quinn's old middle school in Boulder. Sweat, socks, and floor wax. Exactly the same. Quinn didn't know why she was just realizing this now, two months after she'd moved here. Maybe because her adrenaline was pumping. Maybe because all of her senses were in hyperdrive.

"Are you nervous?" Carmen said.

They were sitting on the bleachers, lacing up their sneakers. Quinn was wearing her new ones, first time out. They were blue and white—Gulls Head colors—which might have been a cocky move given that she wasn't on the team yet, but Quinn had been feeling pretty confident at Foot Locker when she picked them out.

"Nervous?" she said. "Nah. I'm pumped."

"Your . . . um . . ." Carmen looked around. There were a bunch of other girls in the gym. Most of them were already shooting. Carm leaned in and whispered in Quinn's ear, "Your wig is crooked."

"It is?" Quinn's hands flew to her head. "Crap."

She grabbed her backpack and ran into the locker room. She shut herself in a stall. It was hard to imagine a worse time for this to be happening. Her hands, she realized as she dug around in the bottom of her backpack for her roll of wig tape, were shaking. She was picturing the worst-case scenario. Sasha flying off in the middle of a layup. Everyone in the gym staring at her. All the girls who were trying out for the team. The coach with her clipboard. The custodian with his mop. Everyone staring at Quinn's bald head, shining under those fluorescent lights.

"Quinn?"

Someone was knocking on the stall.

"It's Carm. Are you okay?"

Was she really supposed to answer that? Of course she wasn't okay. If she was okay, she wouldn't be locked in a bathroom stall two seconds before her tryout.

"Quinn?"

"Yeah." Quinn's nose sounded stuffy. She wasn't crying yet, but it was coming.

"Do you want my lucky bandanna?"

"You have a lucky bandanna?"

"Yeah. It has nothing to do with basketball. It's Red Sox.

I bought it at Big Papi's third-to-last home game, and he signed it."

"Really?"

"Dominican pride, baby. I wear it every time I need good luck . . . Do you need it?"

Quinn looked at Sasha, sitting in her lap. She still hadn't found her wig tape. "Yeah," she said. "I do."

. . . . .

Standing at the foul line, ready to do her best-of-ten, Quinn glanced over at Carmen. Carm pointed at the ceiling, Big Papi style. Quinn could feel the lucky bandanna, snug around her ears. It felt like her dad's hand on her head. Warm. Strong. Sitting on the bleachers behind Carmen were Ivy and Lissa. They were huddled together in a tight knot, watching Quinn.

"Whenever you're ready," the coach said. She was standing under the hoop, holding her clipboard. Short, bushy hair. Whistle around her neck.

"I'm ready," Quinn said.

Bounce, bounce, catch. Bounce, bounce, catch. Elbow. Eyes. Release. Swish.

. . . . .

After dinner that night, Quinn's phone pinged. It was a text from Carm. Did u c the list?

240

Quinn: ???

Carm: The team's posted.

Quinn: Already?

Carm: Check the website. GHHSathletics.edu. Click on girls basketball.

Quinn: Can't u just tell me?

Carm: Nope.

Quinn plugged in the website. She clicked on *Girls' Basketball*. There were ten names listed. Carmen Garcia was number 4. Quinn McAvoy was number 7.

Quinn: OMG!

Carm: OMG OMG OMG!

Quinn: I think it was the lucky bandanna.

Carm: Obv. Jk. It was all u. Welcome to the Gulls.

Quinn: Thx!

Carm: So glad we r teammates.

Quinn: Me too. ☺☺☺☺

Carm: I'm going to text the girls. C u tmrw?

Quinn: Def.

The next person Quinn texted was Nick. Guess what?

Nick: ?

Quinn: I made the team!

Nick: I knew u would. Congrats.

Quinn: Thx.

Quinn: That's not even the best part. I tried out w/o a wig.

Nick: U did?

Quinn: I wore Carmen's lucky bandanna. I guess it worked.

Nick: Way to go.

Quinn: Thx.

Nick: That's a great birthday present.

Quinn: It's not my birthday.

Nick: Ik. It's mine.

Quinn: I missed your birthday????

Nick: Its ok.

Quinn: Y didn't u tell me????

Nick: Idk.

Quinn: I would have made cupcakes.

Nick: U can bake?

Quinn: I am a woman of many talents. What r u doing to celebrate?

Nick: Not much. Family dinner.

Quinn: Meet me @ the beach in the AM? I want to celebrate w/ u.

Nick: U don't have to do that.

Quinn: U don't think making the bball team deserves a celebration?

Nick: Ha ha.

Quinn: Jk. 7:15?

Nick: Ok.

Quinn: Happy birthday.

Nick: Thx.

CHAPTER
23

THE NEXT MORNING, QUINN MADE A DETOUR on her way to the beach. Luckily her skateboard got her from her house to 7-Eleven to the basketball court by 7:15. When Quinn rolled across the beach parking lot, there was Nick, standing on the foul line. Standing.

"Hey," she said, hopping off her board, dropping her backpack on the sand.

"Hey."

She looked around. No wheelchair. No car. "You walked?"

"Yeah."

"Cool." Quinn knew not to make a big deal about it, so she bent over and unzipped her backpack. She could feel Sasha brush against her cheeks. "Here," she said, holding out the package to Nick. "Happy birthday."

Silence. For a moment, she wondered if she'd made a mistake. "I know it's a weird present, but . . ."

"You got me black licorice?"

"Yeah."

"I love black licorice."

"I know. I remembered."

"Thank you." He smiled.

Agh, that smile. Quinn didn't know what to do with that smile. She was sure that Nick could tell it was making her neck hot, her cheeks, her whole head.

She shrugged. "No biggie."

"You want one?" Nick said, tearing open the cellophane and holding out a licorice whip, coiled on his palm like a shiny black snail.

"No thanks," Quinn said, because she hated black licorice. But then she thought about it. The last time she'd actually tried black licorice was when she was little, eating Jelly Bellys at Easter. Maybe her taste buds had evolved. "Aw, what the heck," she said, and popped the black snail into her mouth. It was sweet and spicy and bitter all at once. It made her nose water, just like she remembered. She spat it back into her hand. "Ugh."

Nick laughed. And Quinn realized this was the first time she'd ever heard him laugh. It was like bubbles rising.

. . . . .

After school, a weird thing happened. Quinn went on Instagram to look for this video of a play her old basketball team had invented. "Superslick," they'd called it. Quinn wanted to show it to Carmen. She found the video no problem. It was on Paige's feed, because Paige had been the one recording, and Paige never deleted anything. After Quinn copied the video she started scrolling through Paige's posts, something she hadn't done in months. Quinn came upon a photo of Paige and her mother, their faces pressed close together, smiling the same toothy smile. The caption read, Prayers for my mom, pls. Her cancer is back after 5 years in remission. #cancersucks #devastated.

Quinn's heart stopped right there. She hadn't thought about Paige's mom's cancer since third grade. That was when she'd been diagnosed. That was when she'd had her chemo and her radiation and both her breasts removed. Quinn remembered going over to the Braskys' house with her own mom, bringing casseroles and cookies and flowers. Paige's mom had been amazing through the whole thing. Quinn couldn't remember her crying. She couldn't remember her complaining or saying *Why me?* What Quinn remembered was the day Mrs. Brasky called Paige and Tara and Quinn into her bedroom. "I want you girls to see something," she said. And Paige's mom unbuttoned her shirt to show them the tattoos she'd had inked onto her chest after her mastectomy. Blues and greens and purples and yellows. Flowers and leaves and stars and moons. "When you think of my cancer," Paige's mom said, "I want you to always think of this. Abundant beauty. The gift of life."

That was what Quinn was thinking about right now. Paige's mom's tattoos. How beautiful they were.

I'm so sorry, P, Quinn said in her message to Paige, because no matter what had happened between them, no matter how unfairly Paige had treated her in eighth grade, their friendship went back a long time, all the way to diaper dance. Give your mom a big hug from me. Love, Q.

After Quinn closed out of Instagram, she texted Nick. Can I come over?

Nick: Sure. U ok?

Quinn: Yeah. B there in 20.

She would have asked her mom to drive her, but Mo was at the Cove, attending yet another therapy team meeting to ensure that Julius wasn't planning to BASE jump off any more roofs.

. . . . . .

"I want you to tattoo my head," Quinn said.

Nick's eyebrows shot straight up. It was kind of cute. "Pardon?"

"You heard me," Quinn said. She flung Sasha off and onto Nick's new rug, dark blue to match his new comforter.

"Um . . . ," he said. "I'm not a tattoo artist."

"Not a *real* tattoo. Just . . . you know . . . an ink drawing. With lots of color. It doesn't have to be my whole head. Just whatever you think would look good."

"Whatever I think would look good."

"Yeah. Something abundant and life affirming."

"Abundant and life affirming."

"Is there an echo in here?" Quinn said.

Nick blinked at her.

"I know this is weird, but I don't feel like explaining it right now. Can you just roll with it?"

"Oh, I can roll with it. You've seen me roll."

"Are you making a wheelchair joke?"

"Maybe."

"I've never heard you joke about your wheelchair."

"I've never heard someone ask me to tattoo their head. What kind of pen should I use?"

"I don't know. Any kind."

"Not *any* kind. I don't want to poison you."

Quinn smiled. "You're not going to poison me."

"Your skin is the largest organ in your body. Did you know that?"

"No."

"It's true. And I'm not going to Sharpie the largest organ in your body."

"Just do something small," Quinn said. "I'll survive."

"Small and abundant and life affirming?"

"Yes."

"Right." Nick huffed out a breath. "No pressure."

"No pressure," Quinn said. "No one's going to see this but us."

Nick walked across the room to get his art kit.

Quinn perched on the edge of his bed. "I like your new comforter," she said. "It's spongy."

"I like you sitting down," he said, walking back over, uncapping a pen. "You're making me feel tall."

"Someday you will be."

"Maybe."

"You will," she said. "When you get your new legs with the computerized knees." Quinn lowered her voice. *"Better . . . stronger . . . faster."*

"Have you been watching *The Six Million Dollar Man*?"

She shrugged. "I might have caught another episode."

"Yeah, well. It could be a while before I'm Steve Austin."

"That's okay. It could be a while before my hair grows back."

"Right," Nick said. "I need you to stop talking now. So I can concentrate."

"Okay." Quinn closed her mouth. Her eyes, too.

"Try to stay still."

"Nkay."

When Nick stepped closer she could smell his shirt. Like soap and earth. She could feel his hands on her shoulders, steadying himself. She could feel the tip of his pen on her scalp, just above her left ear, the slightest tickle. Quinn held her breath. She didn't want to laugh.

"You said color, right?" he said.

"Mm-hmm."

Quinn kept her eyes closed as the tickling continued. She heard Nick switch pens. Once. Twice. She lost count of how many switches. She breathed in his smell. She felt the warmth of his chest just inches from her face. She wondered if he could feel her breath.

"Nick?"

"Shhh," he said. "Don't move."

"I'm not moving." Quinn kept her body still and her eyes closed. "That night Julius threw the pizza. When I walked you to the car. You said something that sounded like 'I like juice.' Do you remember that?"

"Yes."

"Is that what you said?"

"No."

"What did you say?"

"You know what I said. Now stop talking. I'm almost done."

Quinn smiled into Nick's shirt.

She had no idea how long it took. But when he was finished, he held up his phone camera so she could see. About two inches above her left ear, stretching its wings wide, was a bird. It was a miniature replica of the bird on his wall, but this one was in color. Purples and golds and greens and blues, each feather blending into the next. It was tiny and delicate and perfect. It was like a jewel, right there on her head.

"I love it," Quinn said.

"You do?"

She looked at him. "It's exactly what I wanted. And I didn't even know what I wanted." She reached into her pocket and pulled out her phone. "Will you take a picture? Just of the bird, not my whole head."

"I like your whole head."

"Well, I like your bird."

Nick took a picture.

"Take a bunch," Quinn said.

He took some more.

"Thank you," she said.

"You're welcome."

When Nick handed back Quinn's phone, their fingers touched. And then, suddenly, they were holding hands. It wasn't at all what Quinn had expected to happen. She was caught off guard, so she said something stupid. "I like your hair, how it wings out on the sides."

Nick smiled. "I like juice."

. . . .

Quinn was rolling down the street on her skateboard, feeling the wind on her face. She hadn't expected any response from

Paige to her Instagram message, because Paige and Tara had basically gone AWOL after she moved. But here was Quinn's phone, pinging in her pocket. Here was Paige's text: Got ur message on ig. It meant a lot to my mom. Thx.

Quinn sat down on the curb and texted back. Ur welcome. How is she?

Paige: Not gr8. She's on a new chemo cocktail. It makes her really tired and nauseous.

Quinn: I'm sry.

Paige: Me too.

Quinn: Tell her I'm thinking abt her.

Paige: I will. Then, for the first time in what—two months?: How r u? Ur fam? Ur new school?

For a second, Quinn considered telling Paige everything: about Gigi's broken hip, and Mo's new studio, and Phil's rules, and Julius up on the roof, and Ivy and Carmen and Lissa, and Nick's legs, and Tommy's nose, and the basketball team, and the bird on her head. She thought about taking a chance and letting Paige in again. But the truth was, Quinn's feet were itching to get back on her skateboard. So she tapped out a quick reply: All's good.

Paige: I'm glad. I really am, Q.

Quinn left it at that. She powered down her phone and hopped back on her board. Maybe she would text Paige tomorrow. But right now, the road was calling her name.

CHAPTER
24

QUINN SAID WHAT SHE NEEDED TO SAY TO GET NICK to the art show on November fifth. She told him that she'd made some art.

It was true, technically. Quinn's fourth-period art teacher, Mr. Diaz, had asked every student in his studio classes to submit something for the show, and Quinn had submitted her self-portrait. This was kind of hilarious because she couldn't draw eyes or noses, or, well, anything resembling a human face, so she had drawn herself from behind. She had drawn her old ponytail, long and thick and hay colored, using three different shades of yellow pastels. And then, because she hadn't known what to do with all the blank space around her head, she'd decided to make it an aquarium. She'd wanted it to look like she was standing in front of the tank, watching the fish. Fish were easy to draw, so she'd made ten of them, all swimming around, one with his mouth open so wide it looked like he was trying to eat her head. Mr. Diaz had laughed when Quinn unveiled her self-portrait to the class. Laughed, out loud, in front of everyone. "No, Quinn, you misunderstand me," Mr. Diaz said when he saw the look on her face. "I'm not laughing in derision. I'm laughing in delight. This is . . . whimsical."

Well, Quinn didn't know how whimsical it was. And she didn't care how many people laughed at her old yellow ponytail hanging on the wall tonight. That wasn't why she was here.

Where was Nick, anyway?

"Do you see Nick?" she asked her mom, who had wanted to come tonight, too, even though Quinn had warned her about the silly self-portrait. Mo insisted on leaving Quinn's dad and Julius at home for a "boys' night" while she and Quinn experienced a "night of culture."

"Mom," Quinn said, pulling her mother away from a sixth grader's lopsided clay pot displayed on a shelf. "Help me find him."

They walked from room to room. Because the art show was grades six through twelve, Mr. Diaz and the middle-school art teacher had needed a lot of wall space, so they were using Gulls Head Congregational Church as their gallery.

"Isn't that Nick over there?" Mo said finally, pointing to the other side of the fellowship hall.

Quinn looked. There he was, wearing a pale blue oxford shirt, hair winging out at the sides. Quinn's stomach did that thing it did now whenever she saw him. It wasn't a flip, exactly. It was more like a slow roll.

Nick didn't notice Quinn. He was saying something to Tommy, who had his arm around a dark-haired girl in a strapless black dress. Quinn knew who this was because Nick had told her. This was Marisol, the Brazilian exchange student. Tommy had asked her out as soon as he was ungrounded. Marisol was beautiful, Quinn had to admit, wide-eyed and pouty-lipped, with long, shiny curls. Well . . . good for Tommy.

Quinn raised an arm and managed to get Nick's attention. Nick waved. Quinn gestured for him to come over.

Mo wandered off to examine more lopsided pots.

It took a while for Nick to roll his way across the room. There were a lot of art gawkers to navigate around. He had to stop. Wait. Say excuse me. Back up. Stop again. *Why the wheelchair?* Quinn found herself thinking. *Why not the legs?*

He finally rolled up to her. "Hey."

"Hey."

"Good turnout."

"Yeah." Quinn looked around, feeling her new Red Sox cap, snug around her ears.

Nick rocked back in his seat, popped a wheelie.

"I have to ask," she said.

"What?"

Quinn opened her mouth. The words were right there on her tongue. She wanted to know. She really, really did. But then it hit her. Asking Nick *Why the wheelchair?* would be like him asking her *Why the hat?* Sometimes Quinn just felt like wearing a hat instead of a wig. Like tonight, she just didn't feel like dealing with wig tape, and she didn't want to have to explain her choice to anyone. Maybe that's how it was for Nick. Maybe he just felt like using his chair at the art show. Maybe tomorrow he'd put on his legs.

"Are you ready to have your world rocked?" she said.

Nick smiled. "You're that good of an artist, huh?"

"Follow me."

It took a while to find what Quinn was looking for. There were so many walls, so many people to steer around. They had to pass Quinn's self-portrait on their way. She wasn't surprised when Nick laughed. She didn't mind. And she didn't mind that he wanted to take a picture with his phone, of Quinn in her new Red Sox cap, standing next to her old yellow ponytail getting eaten by fish. That wasn't why they were here.

"Come on," she said. "I need to show you something."

"Wasn't that it?"

"Nope."

They wove through the bodies. Wove and wove until Quinn finally spotted it: the blue frame. She'd picked it out special.

"There," she said.

"Where?"

Quinn pointed five feet in front of her.

Nick pushed his wheels forward. Pushed again. "Is that . . . ?"

"Yeah." She smiled at the wall. She couldn't stop smiling.

It was Nick's bird, shimmering like a jewel. It was Quinn's head, just the smallest rectangle of bare skin. So small, if you didn't know what it was, you wouldn't know. It was a secret, like the dozens of tiny hairs that were just starting to sprout up under Quinn's Red Sox cap. She hadn't told anyone about the hairs yet, not even Nick. Later, she would. But not now.

" '*Bird in Flight*,' " Nick said, reading off the placard on the wall. " 'By anonymous.' " He looked at Quinn. "Anonymous, huh?"

"You said you don't do shows."

"I don't."

"Well, then."

"Thank you," Nick said. His voice came out gruff, but Quinn knew he wasn't mad. He was the opposite of mad. He reached out his hand and she took it. "Come here," he said. She let him pull her backward, into his lap.

Quinn inhaled. Quinn exhaled. She could smell his smell. She could feel the warmth of his body through her jeans.

He didn't hug her or anything, just rested his arms on the armrests.

They were both quiet. After a minute, he said, "Don't worry. No one's looking at us."

"I don't care if they are," Quinn said. She leaned back against his chest.

He wrapped his arms around her. "Is this okay?"

"Yeah," she said.

They sat there, just the two of them, looking up at Nick's bird, feeling the flutter of wings.

ACKNOWLEDGMENTS

THANK YOU to my incredible editor, Joy Peskin, who continues to challenge me to be a better writer, no matter how many drafts it takes.

Thanks to my agent, Rebecca Sherman, for her steadfast support from the wings, to Morgan Dubin and Johanna Kirby, for their publicity and marketing prowess, and to Elizabeth H. Clark, for her amazing cover design.

To Doodle Barton, Mary Baker, Danielle Gross, Kelli Marcellus, Paige Bean, Karen Holcomb, Kate Anthony, and anyone else who ever held a séance in my living room during a sleepover, thank you for summoning all the best spirits.

Thanks to my meditation mamas—Kerry, Dori, Katie, Happy, Mags, Stephanie, Jen, Tracy, and Sarah—for listening to me vent and reminding me to breathe.

Happy Marino, you get double thanks for sharing your

knowledge of autism, especially the alternative therapies. You are a gem.

Thank you to Dr. David Antonetti for allowing me to pepper him with questions about traumatic crushing injuries and bilateral transfemoral amputations while he was trying to coach baseball.

To my students at Farr ("Fah") Academy, for teaching me to appreciate a wicked Boston accent.

Thank you to Sue Anthony, *magister meus, miris Latine.*

To my college art professor, who laughed at my self-portrait and then apologized to me later, in a note he sent through campus mail: thanks for the story material.

Thank you to the beautiful Sanah Jivani, who sent me a letter when she was fifteen that was so brave and powerful I had to write this book.

Thank you to Kuj, and Jack, and Ben, and Emma—my home team—for keeping the cheers and pizza coming.

Thank you to my parents, Barbara and George, for teaching me to love words. How could I not become a writer?

DON'T MISS THESE OTHER BOOKS BY NATASHA FRIEND!

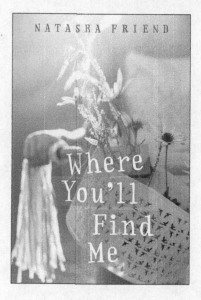

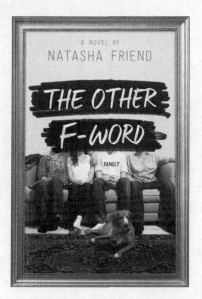